Praise for *The German Money*

"Lev Raphael writes of love, redemption, and revenge with an unflinching honesty that is rare and beautiful. This is an exquisite portrayal of a troubled family, of three siblings each affected differently, but painfully, by their mother's past. A poignant reminder that we cannot hide from history no matter how fast and far we run, *The German Money* is a true and powerful triumph."

—Binnie Kirshenbaum, Author of *Hester Among the Ruins*

THE
GERMAN
MONEY

Also by Lev Raphael

FICTION

Dancing on Tisha B'Av
Winter Eyes

MYSTERIES

Let's Get Criminal
The Edith Wharton Murders
The Death of a Constant Lover
Little Miss Evil
Burning Down the House

NON-FICTION

Edith Wharton's Prisoners of Shame
Journeys & Arrivals
Dynamics of Power (with Gershen Kaufman)
Stick Up For Yourself! (with Gershen Kaufman and Pamela Espe-
    land)
Teacher's Guide to Stick Up For Yourself ! (with Gershen Kaufman and
    Pamela Espeland)
Coming Out of Shame (with Gershen Kaufman)

THE GERMAN MONEY

A Novel by

Lev Raphael

Leapfrog Press
Wellfleet, Massachusetts

Published in 2003 in the United States by
The Leapfrog Press
P.O. Box 1495
95 Commercial Street
Wellfleet, MA 02667-1495, USA
www.leapfrogpress.com

Distributed in the United States by
Consortium Book Sales and Distribution
St. Paul, Minnesota 55114

Printed in Canada

First Edition

Library of Congress Cataloging-in-Publication Data

Raphael, Lev.
The German money : a novel / by Lev Raphael.-- 1st ed.
p. cm.
ISBN 0-9679520-0-X
1. Jews--New York (State)--New York--Fiction. 2. Children of
Holocaust survivors--Fiction. 3. Mothers--Death--Fiction. 4. New York
(N.Y.)--Fiction. 5. Jewish families--Fiction. I. Title.
PS3568.A5988G47 2003
813'.54--dc21
                                    2003001639

10 9 8 7 6 5 4 3 2 1

for B., again and again

"The living room, the most treacherous country of all."
—Elizabeth Benedict, *Safe Conduct*

THE
GERMAN
MONEY

I used to think that some people had a true gift for life, more than just a talent or even a skill. Call it a richness of being. While others, like my family, like me, were paupers, doomed to struggle against their own inner poverty.

I was wrong, of course—but then there's always a story if you think you can see around corners.

Here's where mine begins: I actually thought I was lucky when my mother died. I was alone, in another state, and I knew nothing about the money she had left me, the German money, we had always called it, reparations for her years in Nazi concentration camps.

I had escaped to a small cabin on the western shore of Old Mission Peninsula, lent to me by a fellow librarian at the University of Michigan. Old Mission is one of the more isolated spots in northern Michigan. Stretching up from Traverse City, this thin strip of rolling hills cuts Grand Traverse Bay in half and the 36-mile drive around the peninsula is one of Michigan's most romantic.

It was a perfect hideaway in a place I'd often imagined sharing with Valerie, the woman I'd dated in college and should have married. But I'd stupidly fled New York and her years ago, so that was impossible.

Michigan's winter tends to start well before Thanksgiving, and though many people are weary of it by late March, I wasn't. The time just before the buds grew large was one I loved most, when the nude trees stood out starkly against the snowy ground and the dove-gray skies, more compelling than any sculpture could be. There was no trace of real color yet and you were wrapped in amazing gradations of gray and brown—like living in a Braque collage. Even the sunsets were muted, and every second of true attention and silence revealed subtle textures and a kind of wealth that stills the mind.

I disconnected the cabin's phone, shut off my cell phone and hardly even talked to the friendly cashiers when I drove down to the huge mall market twenty minutes south in Traverse City that was a glare of food, appliances, drugs and sale clothing, to pick up fish, steak, and thick soups.

The drive north to Traverse, up 27, up to the hills and farms and then west on two-lane roads, had stripped from me people, time, words. I read very little that weekend, never listened to the CD player I had almost forgotten to bring. Mostly I just walked up and down the hills or along the shore, satisfied and quiet. The cabin was as bland, as characterless as a worn-out doll without clothes, hair or eyes—so getting out wasn't just pleasurable, it was a must.

From the highest ridge on the peninsula, I could see both arms of the bay and imagine Lake Michigan further west. Despite its size, Lake Michigan is finished, bounded: you can comprehend it in your mind as well as on a map. Even though I grew up in New York City, the Atlantic has always seemed more like an *idea* of a body of water to me, a theory or example.

Once, maybe twice, I thought about the phone message I'd received about a week before from my mother, the first one in years. There was no greeting, no content, no request for a return call, just the blunt statement "This is your mother." As if there was a doubt I'd recognize her voice no matter how infrequently I heard it. At first I was startled, then puzzled, then angry. Why was she calling? And why couldn't she have left a real message?

I didn't call back. I was terrible at answering messages, but if I'd stayed home in Ann Arbor an extra day or not shut off my cell, I would have gotten my brother Simon's calls telling me my mother had died, and I'd have flown to New York.

Simon had to handle everything, because our sister Dina, furious at her husband Serge, had flung her cell phone under a truck, and stormed off to sit in the bar of Quebec City's Hotel Frontenac, drink a whole bottle of Veuve Clicquot, smoke half a pack of DuMauriers, and flirt with her waiter—a set of rituals she indulged in whenever she was irate.

Simon went ahead with our mother's funeral on his own, helped by Mrs. Gordon, a new neighbor of hers I'd never met, but who seemed to have become very close.

"Mrs. Gordon saved me," Simon kept repeating. And who else could have? We had no close relatives alive and most of my parents' friends had died or retired to Florida.

I didn't know the woman, but I felt jealous, and stung. Why was this stranger making such a difference?

My younger brother functioned well in emergencies he hadn't created, but afterwards would grind himself down with criticism, a slave to what he *should* have done. Looking at his slim frame and youthful face you'd never have guessed he harbored such internal savagery. All the disasters that had soiled his life seemed a fulfillment of some kind—as if the ugliness he felt inside could only be given outward expression in divorce, debt, scandal, and utter failure.

I was isolated and unreachable while Simon went ahead with the funeral and Dina sulked in retreat from the latest in a series of men who couldn't give her what she longed for. My sister had made a confused career of rage—trailing broken windows, torn clothes, lipstick scrawls on bathroom mirrors from man to man, or so she said, a little proudly. They generally forgave her, at least the ones she allowed to.

That lasted until she got married seven years ago to Serge, a rich and unrelenting Québécois who looked like a Gallic Pierce Brosnan. For many reasons, it was a difficult marriage, and I knew that just from the little Dina told me. His holy terror of a mother despised his having married not just an English speaker and a non-Catholic, but a *Jew*, one of the Devil's own. Serge and the other Gilberts were a fierce and proud clan, tracing their lineage back to the founders of New France in Canada. Anything Dina did that Serge disliked was apparently the subject of censure by sisters, brothers, aunts, uncles, cousins, probably even baby sitters and maybe commiserating neighbors, too. When Serge argued with Dina, he carried himself like a broker representing his entire investment house—backed by its power, authority, tradition.

This corporate disapproval was new for Dina. Men had always succumbed to her tantrums, because she was a knockout: curly blonde hair, gray eyes, sexily slim theatrical body and voice, a presence more than a woman. Dina had tried acting in college, but the lights, sets, costumes, and makeup had diminished her somehow, forced her into unaccustomed calculation.

Dina's the beautiful one, Simon is messed up, and I'm the brain—at least that's how we thought of ourselves, which tells you a lot doesn't it? We were stick figures, not people.

When I left Old Mission and drove the five hours back to Ann Arbor to find Simon's phone messages and telegram, I felt protected by the silence I always discovered up north, from my walks down the beach at the tip of the Peninsula (which was half way between the North Pole and the Equator), the clear nights gaping at the Milky Way and a wilderness of stars, afternoons dozing on the sun-beaten couch, three days of solitude and rest.

The German Money

I played my brother's messages standing in my bedroom, looking out at the quiet street. His voice sounded thinner and more nasal than usual. Spring was a little closer down here than up north, but winter was still in command, having stripped the large maples and oaks of their leaves long ago. My view was framed and laced by dramatic, jagged bare tree limbs, thrust into a prominence they deserved. This neighborhood was full of 100-year old trees, and in the late fall and winter, driving or walking its streets was like entering a vast quirky sculpture hall.

In Michigan I often felt the seasons form a kind of pentimento, with one peering out from under another. Maybe because I'd fallen in love with the state and its history, through travel and through reading, and so often mused on the larger cycles of time. The ways in which over the centuries trappers were succeeded by loggers, then miners, and after them the men building cars, and how certain towns in the state were still identified with one industry, sometimes even after it had moved on. I could easily picture the snaking dusty Indian trails giving way, in time-lapse photography, to the log roads and ultimately the grim highways.

Looking out the window at the bare trees, with Simon's messages a weird kind of white noise, I could hear people on tractor mowers sucking up leaves to dump in ragged soft piles by the road to be hauled off by huge noisy trucks, and smell the tang of leaves from the few driveways where they were being burned (illegally) that seemed to have infiltrated my comfortable apartment.

Listening to the answering machine message again and again, I heard about my mother's sudden death, heard Simon's requests for support and advice, heard how the funeral—which according to the Jewish tradition Simon refused to violate—had to be within twenty-four hours, and Dina's hysterics when she found out. Through each grim recital, I felt a tranquility as deep as the grief I would have expected to feel.

I was surprised at her heart attack because my mother had always been in perfect health, at least I thought so, remembering her brisk walks along Manhattan's Riverside Drive. And she'd once boasted that she had the heart of a woman half her age.

But I wasn't frightened or depressed. That was probably the difference my solitary weekend on Old Mission had made for me. I did not feel, as Simon probably did, finally thrust into a grim adulthood, orphaned; or like Dina, deprived of a reality that had shaped her revolt. If anything, I was calm. I felt ready, and preparing to fly to New York to be with my brother and sister—who I hadn't seen in over five years—I kept thinking how lucky I was that the worst was over.

· · · · ·

"Cremation would have made more sense," Dina said when we came back to Simon's apartment in Forest Hills from the vast stone and grass death park in New Jersey. I was startled by the blaze of her beauty, heightened by the elegant black Armani suit and heels that had a vaguely foreign edge to them. With a mass of blonde curls, Dina had the looks of one of those rosy, dreamy-eyed angels playing a lute in a Renaissance fresco, and she had always carried herself differently from her friends, back straighter, head higher, yet without a sense of strain. The first time I traveled to Paris, I realized she had somehow picked up the kind of grace and self-possession you see in women around the Place Vendôme or on the Rue de Rivoli. She had enviable chic and I had seen women on buses or subways in New York scan her up and down, sullenly looking for a flaw.

That gauntlet was nothing compared to what she grew up with. Our mother criticized her relentlessly: Dina was never good enough, never pretty enough, never stylish enough. She would badger Dina about her hair being too long or too short, her makeup being too flashy or too subtle, damn the colors she chose, the styles she wore or discarded—even her nail polish. "Leave her alone!" Dad would say, but it was barely a suggestion, more the good-humored, disinterested chiming-in of a kibitzer watching a card game. My mother not only criticized the shape of Dina's eyebrows when she plucked them (and when she didn't), she went further, deeper: "You'll never keep a man. Nobody will want you." These slaps were delivered with the matter-of-fact brutality of a disgusted coach calling his team "wimps" (or worse), but I never believed my mother was trying to harshly inspire Dina. It felt more like punishment. Dina fought back, but her rage was desperate—the last response of a defeated population to its triumphant invaders. And almost always, she was quelled or fled crying to her room. Later, she learned to stare our mother down, but between them that was not a triumph, only a deadly silent draw.

"Cremation," Dina repeated.

I had felt alien there at the cemetery in that broad glistening sea of tombstones, wave after wave of carved Hebrew swirling around me, heavily reminding me that I was no more substantial than the small rocks or pebbles that people left on the monuments to mark their visits. I never understood this Jewish custom, which no book had seemed to adequately explain to me. And it seemed pointless—didn't the stones fall off? Despite the gesture, nothing was changed, nothing achieved. People left the scene of this vain effort just as separate, confused, and thrust apart by what always sundered them: the knowledge that all of us would end up here, or someplace like it.

I hated not knowing exactly where to stand because every square inch of ground seemed given over to graves. In my awkward progress from the parking lot to my mother's grave I could have been a little kid trying to step across hot sand. Now and then the carving on a tombstone, or the glint of sunlight on dark polished granite, or simply the music of a name in English had reached me, but otherwise I felt overwhelmed, crushed.

So many lives, so many names. I suddenly remembered Valerie once joking that when we died, we could have side-by-side graves marked 'His' and 'Hers.'

"But that means we'd be married," I had blurted out, and she turned away.

At the cemetery, I thought, my mother is buried out here, but the words weren't any more meaningful than an advertising slogan you glimpse on the side of a bus. And Dina, Simon, and I were like strangers drawn by curiosity to the scene of a minor accident, not mourners. I avoided glances from anyone we passed, not wanting them to see how little was in my eyes. I was dead, too.

If the barren grave site had made me dizzy, it silenced us all on the hour and a half ride back to Forest Hills cutting through the city in dense traffic that stunned me after the relative quiet of Michigan. Even driving on the highways around Detroit at 85 miles per hour—if you didn't want to be cut off—wasn't this chaotic and oppressive, perhaps because there wasn't the heavy dull backdrop of brick and concrete there, seemingly about to tumble across the lanes of cars. New York struck me as resentful and lurking, ready to fall.

As usual, Dina was the first to speak when we got upstairs at Simon's. And I winced when she said "cremation." It struck me as crude and disgusting—forget about it being forbidden to Jews. While I may not have been only vaguely Jewish, this taboo was somehow one I'd absorbed very early. Just like the injunction never to do anything shameful that "the *goyim*" would see. My mother never said much about either subject, so my father was the source of both prohibitions, I suppose, but especially the latter. He'd read *The Post* or *The Daily News* and make tsk-tsk-tsk noises if he found a story about a criminal with a Jewish-sounding name. These he read aloud, with dramatic pauses, whether anyone seemed to be paying attention or not. And the fact that a Jew was giving other Jews bad publicity seemed worse to him than the transgression involved, even if it was murder. He had come over from Russia as a boy, but he acted as if Americans were as Jew-crazy as the Russians, waiting for the least excuse to launch a pogrom.

When Dina had said the word "cremation," for me it did not conjure up romantic images of a lover's ashes scattered at sea. All I could think of was hungry, horrible flames.

The three of us were silent for a few moments.

"But Mom was against cremation," Simon objected, looking lost on his florid gold couch. "Wasn't she?"

Dina shrugged. "I never heard her talk about it."

"It's disgusting," he said softly. And I agreed, though I felt distracted.

I had not seen Simon's new one-bedroom apartment before. It was strange, surprisingly vulgar, glittering with fake crystal, slashed with red and gold: like the bad taste of someone who had known poverty, I thought, and found relief in the textures and colors of a child's fantasy castle. The thick drapes were baroquely swagged and festooned. Sitting there drinking coffee from a china cup smeared with shepherdesses, I saw Simon as incomprehensible. How could my brother have chosen to live like this? It was bizarre as if he'd robed himself in hemp and taken to squatting in some musty cave. All this spurious frou-frou must have been left by a previous tenant, and maybe its very completeness was what had attracted my brother, for whom something always seemed to be missing. The apartment was like some wildly improbable shell a hermit crab might have crawled into, especially given the way he looked now.

Simon's blond hair was short and spiky to match a scrap of goatee, and he had on baggy cargo pants, Converse All Stars and an oversized gray sweater whose sleeves hung almost down to his fingers. He looked half his age, not that clothes could have made him seem much older. His voice still had the kind of buzz you hear in adolescent boys, and he had never outgrown the lanky awkwardness of a teenager who seems at war with his own body, fighting its potential for public humiliation. His nose and lips were full for his angular face and he often seemed on the verge of sinking down into himself, hurt green eyes hooded, shoulders falling and back slumping over as if responding to some internal inquisition he could only answer with silence.

"Burn her up? No way. That's what they wanted to do to Mom," Simon went on. "In the War." He didn't add that "they" had done that to everyone else in her family—we didn't need the reminder. If family stories are a meeting place like the atrium of an ancient Roman home where all can gather, then what our home was built around was a darker emptiness: the utter lack of stories, at least from my mother.

Silence, emptiness, loss had always howled through our home. We knew from flickers and hints that my mother had lost everyone and everything, that her village near the Polish city of Vilna (now Lithuania's Vilnius) had been wiped from the earth in a rampage of Nazi burning, shooting, gassing. Centuries of Jewish life there were crushed, extinguished; even tombstones had been ripped from the ground and used to pave roads. And though she was alive, she had not escaped the stench of death or the impress of its dark hand.

Dina frowned now at what Simon was saying.

But he didn't let it rest, he had to lay it out for us. "I couldn't have watched her coffin slide into the flames. It's like the Nazis and all those Jews shoveled into the ovens."

Dina turned away.

I wondered what my mother's death had been like, if my mother had suffered or died instantly, as Simon had been told. Instantly, and with no pain. Heart failure. How can anyone really know what that instant of death had felt like for her?

But these questions didn't open me up—they were dry and theoretical. I couldn't connect them with the freshly dug grave I'd seen just hours before, with our strange isolation in Simon's living room. We hung there like the tassels at his windows: separate, mildly ridiculous—not a real family at all.

"It's sick," Dina charged, unable to sit. "Putting a body in the ground." She paced the room, angry, unseeing, her black dress beautifully wrinkled. Even her uncharacteristically ragged nails and pulled-at hair were attractive, demonstrative: she had the *look* of grief, the confused interruptions. "Then the damned gravestone. All that pretending you can go there and share something."

I agreed with her about that, at least. I thought that Dina wanted to cry, and I might have wanted to hold her, but we weren't that sort of family.

After any kind of absence, my mother had never met us with happy hugs and kisses, or even a smile. Her pale oval face under the dense mound of dark blonde hair that looked as artificial as a bad wig made you think of some nocturnal mammal hiding from its predators. She even wore dark colors as if trying to camouflage herself, though I didn't see any flaws in her figure. Slightly above average height for a woman, she was trim, with small pretty hands and feet, though she never expressed vanity about either, never bragged about her lovely shoes or spent hours reverently caring for her hands.

While Dad would shout a hello that was so hearty it always sounded fake, my mother would stand eyeing us almost warily, as if expecting some kind of betrayal. It was very strange. She was certainly gracious, elegant, but it was a cool and distant charm, quietly self-absorbed (while Dad exhibited a noisy version of the same characteristic). She wasn't going to put herself out for anyone, in any way. Around her, I had often felt like a disobedient courtier crossing a painfully long audience chamber to his monarch's waiting, censorious frown. Her name was Rose (Rushka back home) and it didn't make you think of soft and fragrant petals, but thorns.

Heart failure.

Her heart had failed, had failed *us*, a long time ago. And my father, who had come to America as a little boy but had never lost his Russian-Polish accent, he was not truly any warmer—just loud. The noise level perfectly matched his looks. Short, balding, and skinny, he had the bulbous red nose, thick arched eyebrows and pointy ears you'd expect in a vaudeville comedian. While he looked like a clown, he acted like a bully, and meals in restaurants were a special torment. He'd badger the waiter with hostile questions and jovially try to make us change our orders to something *he* thought we would like better. Not even a deli meal could be peaceful. "Dina, you're sure you want a potato knish? The meat's much better here. And Simon, what's with the pastrami sandwiches all the time—try something different. Try it, you'll like it! Hah-hah-hah."

Our mother had her own ideas about restaurant behavior. If any of us kids chatted with the waiter or made jokes, she would sneer and sharply remind us—when the waiter was gone—that *she* didn't come to restaurants for making friends.

"Cremation," Dina said again, this time speculatively, as if it was the name of some island retreat she was thinking of flying to. She fussed with her black Mikimoto pearls, an anniversary gift from Serge.

I pictured again the chilling row upon row of gravestones—a strange stunted crop in barren soil. In movies, graveyards are either eerie or romantic, filled with bleak twisted trees or full of charming walks and vistas. This one was neither, just a cold metropolis of death.

Dina was upset again. "That's what I'll think of next year when we have to light the *yorzeit* candle for Mom. That we did the wrong thing."

"But you'll light one anyway?" Simon asked, voice cracking. "Won't you?"

"Of course." Dina glanced my way. "How about you?"

I hesitated before saying, "I don't know."

The German Money

Disgusted with my answer, Dina stalked into his bedroom, which Simon had insisted she use, muttering about a nap.

"At least it was quick," Simon said to me, but I didn't want to follow that up in any way. He could have meant our mother's death, and not Dina turning her back on me.

Simon went to the kitchen to start lunch and I sat on his couch. Here we were, together after more than five years, and we'd taken the first chance to get out of each other's company.

I tried interesting myself in a magazine. Through the closed door of Simon's bedroom, I could hear a radio on very low, and I remembered how years ago, our family dinners had often ended with someone angry, someone silent, someone off in another room. I used to dread the holidays that forced us even closer, and birthdays, too. All five of us had been born in June and July so those two months were a fever of cards and plans and disappointments. My mother usually returned what we got her or put it away in her closet. Dad would cheerfully open his presents, announce with counterfeit delight what they were and then set them aside. Nothing we bought pleased either one of them, or seemed to. Why?

They usually gave all three of us money, suggesting appropriate gifts we could buy for ourselves. It was cold and somehow demeaning, as if we were hired help getting a bonus we were too stupid to spend on our own.

And us? Dina laughed at her presents, out of embarrassment, I think. Simon was often quiet, reflective; and I tore wrappings and boxes open with a hunger that still surprises me because it hasn't faded. I don't know what I was looking for.

Would I light a memorial candle for my mother next year to commemorate her death? I had never done that before, never had the need to, and observing the ritual struck me as quietly outlandish—like having to learn a whole new language overnight. As a family, we hadn't been very demonstrably Jewish. An orphan when he came to America, Dad had been raised by socialist cousins, which left him with hearty contempt for Judaism, and we all assumed that our mother's War years had made her even more resolutely a-religious. Our parents had contributed to Jewish charities, bought Israeli bonds, but the holidays had been ignored or hardly observed. And Simon and I had never been pressured to study for a bar mitzvah—how could they have pushed us, when they never went to synagogue or even talked about taking us there?

My parents hadn't had Simon and me circumcised either, as if even a metaphor were too great a commitment to the past. I had never discussed this with Simon, but I know that it had the unintentional result of livening up my sex life. My ex-girlfriend Camilla, for one, had been grateful: "It's a Happy Meal!"

Despite not being ritually scarred like other Jewish men—isn't the dark band that circumcision leaves a kind of wedding ring?—Simon and I, like Dina, had flirted with "being Jewish." Simon read books about the Holocaust; I studied Yiddish authors in translation for a year or so, briefly contemplating doing Jewish studies somewhere. In high school, Dina was involved in collecting for so many charities that we mocked her as Saint Dina. But none of it lasted, and our parents didn't seem to care; Dad, an accountant, had just wanted to support us.

I don't know what my mother wanted. But her indifference gave way to occasional odd flashes of hostility, and I do know that she loathed Simon's reading about the Holocaust, though she never said a word. For an awful year in high school, Simon gulped down every book he could find about the concentration camps, and in the bedroom we shared, books stamped with swastikas, barbed wire, blood-red titles, and broken Stars of David leered at me, brutal, deranged. I avoided the subject, which was easy for me.

Dina would explode at Simon: "Don't read that stuff—it's over! It's crazy!"

Simon said he had to. But if he was doing it to understand

why our mother never discussed her War years, or to please our mother, or simply to reach her, she refused the offering and resolutely ignored him whenever he was reading something about the Holocaust and tried to talk about it. I thought it was cruel of him in a way, when she wanted so desperately to forget. In contrast, hers was the cruelty of silence.

I don't know what my brother learned through all his reading and I never asked Dina if he shared any of it with her. The darkness of my mother's past was too frightening for me—like Dina, like my mother, I sought only to push it away. I was glad she said nothing, shared nothing.

I had been fleeing those horrors since the day during recess in kindergarten when I heard an older girl, who was teaching another one a complicated dance step, say offhandedly that Germans picked Jewish babies up by the feet and cracked their skulls against walls. "Like eggs," she said confidently, pigtails flapping as she spun and turned. I could see my mother making us pancakes and skillfully breaking eggs with one hand into a bright blue bowl. I shuddered.

Where had the girl heard this? On television? From her parents?

And I had immediately thought of little Simon—who as a one-year-old still seemed half-baby blanket, half-mouth to me—flung against the playground wall. I fled the roiling chaos of my stomach, but I didn't make it to the cavernous, cool boys' room with its huge opaque windows, humiliating myself just inside the entrance's heavy double doors.

Through the warm attention of my teacher Miss Lerman and the bus ride home with my mother, who'd been called to pick me up, I had felt dizzy, chilled. Bed didn't help, or warm Coca-Cola, or a story. Only sleep saved me that raw afternoon when I was five years old.

My mother thought it was the flu, so had Miss Lerman. I told no one what I'd heard, not even Valerie, years later, because her parents were both Holocaust survivors. I couldn't tell her—it would have brought us as unbearably close, I saw, as conspirators fleeing their crime.

That day in Simon's apartment after our return from the cemetery, I wondered at my years of silence, and my mother's, which were so much more mysterious.

· · · · ·

Simon's lunch was delicious: cream of broccoli soup, a Spanish omelet, apple pie. Dina liked eating Simon's cooking and they hugged before sitting at the dinette table. I resented their closeness in a flash of remembered annoyance. While I still lived at home, in Manhattan, I used to come back to find them talking and laughing in Dina's room, finishing each other's sentences, happy as lovers. When they'd invite me to sit down and enjoy a record album, I felt patronized, excluded, more like a little brother than the eldest.

"So eat," Simon urged now, trying to be funny, imitating our father.

Nothing had changed. Simon used his fingers as a knife to push his food around, and Dina cut her food into smaller and smaller portions as if trying to make it disappear.

We ate without speaking. I thought of my mother's favorite print: a Diego Rivera painting of a man bent almost to the ground under the weight of an impossibly heavy basket on his back. I felt that same heaviness sinking deeper and deeper inside of me, implacable. I wondered about this print. Would Simon or Dina want it? Did I? What would it remind me of?

We sat like huddled survivors of a flood thankful for their Red Cross bowl of soup. But that was nothing new. Our meal times, even family car trips to the Cloisters, to Hyde Park, Montauk Point, had often seemed provisional, a gathering of threatened strangers who knew that each other's company was no guarantee of safety. Was it our mother's past, the gaping emptiness in the center of our home that was like a meteor crater, one so vast that we could never even make a transit of its perimeter?

"When I heard Mom was dead, I cried until I was sick," Dina broke out. "But it didn't change anything. I didn't feel better, just exhausted."

Simon nodded.

Dina's words plunged me back into a strange memory: I saw myself at three or four, hysterical, sobbing hopelessly in the hallway outside a gleaming black apartment door, knowing I would not be let in until my mother was ready—or never. It was the same. She had wildly plucked me from my chair in the kitchen and thrust me into the hall, slamming the black door as heavy as stone. What had I done or said? I couldn't remember.

"What about you?" Dina asked, startling me. "You haven't been crying, have you?"

I shrugged, saying I hadn't felt anything much.

"Figures," Dina snapped, spearing some egg with her fork.

"What's *that* mean?"

She flushed. "Aren't you ever going to thaw out?"

"You're upset," Simon murmured, clearing his place.

Dina stared at me, even prettier with her face flushed and tight. What was I supposed to do? Yell at her? Tell her she was wrong? Shake her?

I left the table, grabbed my coat, and went for a walk. Though it's nothing like Ann Arbor, Forest Hills is mildly pleasant for a New York neighborhood, with street after street of red brick apartment buildings of all sizes, everywhere scraps of lawn, bushes, well-pruned trees. It's all so careful, clean, and well-tended that Queens Boulevard's eight lanes slash through like a gross and dangerous joke. We were actually not that far from the Queens neighborhood where Kitty Genovese had been raped and killed in the early 1960s and no one had come to her aid even though the nightmare, the screaming and stabbing, went on for hours. To me, this symbolized New York every bit as much as the Statue of Liberty.

Sitting on a bench in a tiny concrete triangle studded with trees, I took the sun for a while with ranks of bundled up old and elderly Jews chatting in Russian, Yiddish and other languages I couldn't recognize. My mother would never have a quiet old age, I thought, as a Q60 bus with great staring windows heaved past. And I felt hot with shame, exposed. I couldn't even remember the last time I'd seen my mother or recall anything from our last conversation—how long ago had that been? And thinking of a phrase my mother used, I hadn't even "found it for necessary" to return the first call she'd made to me in years.

At the cemetery, on the grim drive back, at lunch, I'd been tempted to ask about my mother's heart disease. Was she taking anything for it? Did they know? Was she being treated? How long had she been ill, and why hadn't they told me? But the questions felt like a trap that would ensnare me in Dina's outrage and Simon's frustration at having had the funeral all to himself, even though he didn't have to scramble to set it up.

"That was thoughtful of Mom," Dina had said more than once, almost puzzled. "Setting up the funeral arrangements and paying for it all. Years ago. That's what I would do."

I wasn't sure if it was thoughtfulness or not wanting us to be involved in making any decisions, not wanting us to screw it up. Apparently one call from Simon had set things in motion, but he had been the one forced to choose clothes for our mother and see the body taken away, and in his more than usually fraught silence I felt his resentment stab at both of us—me especially since I was the eldest—for not having been there to support him. I had trouble looking him in the face now, because he was right to be aggrieved.

I had been so contented, at peace on Old Mission as the life had left my mother's body. My absence seemed disgraceful to me, unforgivable. If they knew, I thought, almost afraid to look at the men and women around me. I hadn't seen my mother in more than five years and she was dead.

The noise, the heat, the scrape of shopping cart wheels, the tangle of languages and heavily accented English, the sense of "The Bullvar" (as I had heard people around me pronounce it) as an endless scar, even the pretty clouds hemmed me in.

Though everyone said that the city was safer and cleaner than it had been in years, New York made no sense to me after a decade and a half of living in Michigan. I couldn't experience the excitement, the power I was supposed to feel and enjoy in this city—I only knew the noise, the oppression, the stifling weight of it all. Had I ever really imagined that there was no other place in the world to live?

Our parents moved us down to the Upper West Side when I was starting junior high school, but we'd grown up in Inwood at the northern tip of Manhattan in a German-Jewish neighborhood shadowed by Inwood Hill Park filled with old Indian caves that had been carved by glaciers thousands of years ago and where you could still find Indian arrowheads. We kids had loved discovering pieces of mica schist and peeling off its shiny layers. That park was a mysterious place with 200-year-old oaks, a retreat where the city below was not just distant but invisible, an oasis whose silence mocked the city's noise like the call of the crows in the hundred feet high canopy. There were the quirky gingko trees—with their fan-like pulpy leaves—that were originally from China. As a little boy, this had seemed miraculous to me—trees from the other side of the world.

It had all been clean and quiet and close enough by subway to where things really happened: Downtown. But even before Inwood decayed as the city around it seemed to smear itself with filth, before New York had begun to seem impossible and crazy, before we moved down to the cleaner and safer Upper West Side, I had been ready to leave, ready for a new home. And now, fifteen years after I'd left New York, the city seemed more unbearable than ever. Leafing through the New York Times, I'd felt the city's fabled cultural richness as overwhelming, like a devilish list that would grow longer and more demanding no matter what you crossed off it.

I had not thought of myself as a New Yorker in years. When people asked where I was from, I always said Michigan. I suppose I could also have said "nowhere," but that would have been rude.

I didn't have a New York accent anymore, so the fraud was believable. I said "sack" for paper bag, "pop" for soda, though I drew the line at such local variants as "heighth" and "acrosst." I understood that you located unfamiliar places in Michigan for other Michiganders by showing your hand and pointing because it was vaguely the mitten shape of the Lower Peninsula. I said "Michiganders" rather than the pretentious though official "Michiganians." I followed and reveled in the football rivalry between the University of Michigan and Ohio State, as well as the in-state rivalry with Michigan State. I had been desperate to fit in, or more accurately, to disappear.

Maybe I'd succeeded too well.

Picturing the bare-dirt grave, I imagined my own burial. Who would come—who would care?

Just then I noticed that the well-bundled old people on the bench across from me were smiling at me with the greedy benevolence of residents at a nursing home spotting someone else's visitor. They looked so hungry I wanted to shout, "Fuck you! Leave me alone!"

I hurried away from my bench.

Forest Hills was very clean (even for the revitalized New York), and walking back to Simon's apartment along the pavement that seemed to conjure against the city's dirt, I saw that the three of us weren't much different than the children we had been. I remembered Dina shouting and stomping her little feet, Simon offering one of his toys, infant appeaser, and me unable to do anything but flee. Dina's anger was like the shrill of birds in a pet store—pure noise, hard to find meaningful; it had always driven me off.

In the small cheaply-paneled elevator, it was obvious to me that I'd never much liked Dina and I didn't know Simon well enough to be sure. God, we were a sorry bunch.

Upstairs, Simon apologized.

"What for?"

"Dina. She's upset."

"She's not upset. She's turning into Mom. I always thought she wanted to be the opposite, but look at her."

Simon shrugged, not willing to agree or disagree. He watched me unpack and lay my things out in a corner of the garish living room. I grinned at that tactful word "upset," wondering how I was supposed to talk to him; Dina was usually our go-between. That is, when she wasn't pissed off at me or Serge or the world.

"Mom called me a week before she died," I said.

Simon's face was expressionless but his voice showed his surprise. "What did she say?"

"Nothing. It was just a message on my machine. Did she tell you she was going to call me?"

He shrugged. "No." He looked as puzzled as if I'd told him that the Pope had left me a message. My mother had never been one for staying in touch—at least with me.

When I sat on the couch, Simon asked if he could say something. I shrugged and he joined me, eyes bruised, confiding, but he didn't speak, and I waited a bit nervously. Simon had been through so many fires: drugs, drifting, car accidents, addiction, divorce. He scared me. There was something almost historical about failure so sustained. Looking at him, it was hard not to feel our parents' disappointment that all he'd done with his life was become—at thirty-five—a cab driver. I could imagine my father's derisory, "Immigrants do that—people who don't speak English. You're an American!"

31

Cab driving was not what my father had meant when he urged all of us as children to "Do something practical, like me! Numbers, numbers you can count on!" The unspoken message was that the suffering he'd escaped in Eastern Europe, the suffering he at most only alluded to as "terrible—don't ask" awaited each one of us if we didn't follow his advice.

We knew his father had been killed in some kind of pogrom and that his mother had died of TB. "She died in my arms," was all he ever told us. He was only ten or eleven (the story often changed), and distant cousins in New York brought the orphan to a new home that wasn't anybody's idea of the promised land. Well-to-do owners of a men's clothing store, they gave him a dark, tiny maid's room in their enormous Washington Heights apartment, and treated him like a servant, mocking his accent when he learned English, his hopes to better himself, everything. Stingy and mean-hearted, they consistently punished him for *their* lack of benevolence, and as soon as he graduated high school, he escaped.

"It was like a prison," was one of his few dark comments. "Those sons of bitches." He had worked as a delivery boy, a pants presser and who knew what else. But since he had been able, finally, to make a very good living for his family, it was obvious to my father that he was right when he gave us advice.

My mother had her own message, at least for me. In grade school I'd been enamored of school trips to the zoo and nature walks and proud that my compositions and reports about these events were praised by my teachers. My mother approved of the grades but not of the assignments. "Writing—what will it get you?" She said it enough times to shred my barely formed dreams of writing, of writing books about what I saw in the world when I was very quiet. And so I had become a glorified custodian of other people's books, afraid to read writers like Annie Dillard or even Thoreau because I might feel jealous and ashamed. She had crushed me, unlike Dina, who responded to our mother's constant criticism by devoting herself to becoming irresistible to others.

"Paul?" Simon asked at last. "Are you scared?"

I nodded carefully, since I felt that was the required answer. You learn that with women: don't commit yourself by saying anything until you see where the conversation is headed. And even then. . . .

"I can't sleep. Driving my cab makes me crazy. Dina can't help."

"Dina. She needs too much attention."

"We all do. 'Attention—attention must be paid.' Remember?"

I did, unpleasantly so. Years ago Simon and I had seen a revival of *Death of a Salesman* and gotten drunk afterwards talking about Dad. Simon told me how Dad always made him feel he wasn't good enough, which was funny because I thought Dad let him off the hook too easily. That night, in the bedroom we shared, Simon had crept from his bed to hold me. All night he hugged me fiercely in his sleep, like he did when we were little boys, muttering once something that might have been, "Don't let them get me." I felt embarrassed and even angry with him, but didn't have the heart to kick him out—he was so pathetic.

And years later, when he came out to Dina, then me, as bisexual, it struck me as even more embarrassing because I'd wondered if part of his need for comfort was erotic. It tainted the memory even more.

The morning after the play, Simon had looked ashamed of himself and wouldn't talk to me, which I found a relief. It was not an episode I wanted to relive in any way.

"I'm so tired," he said now, leaning on my shoulder and then putting his head down on my thigh. I was tired, too, and didn't pull away. Who the fuck cared any more?

While he was asleep, I debated about it, and then gave way, stroking his hair once or twice, since he was asleep. I figured it couldn't be misinterpreted, and it seemed the thing to do.

Oddly, I found myself wishing I could cry for the mother we had lost and maybe never had.

When Dina emerged from having napped, she smiled at the fraternal Pietà, and I felt like a jerk. She called an old college friend and invited herself over for dinner, while Simon and I headed for a nearby deli and gobbled kosher franks and steaming, crisp-skinned potato knishes. We reminisced in the featureless but redolent deli about childhood Friday nights when Dad would celebrate the end of the week by arriving home with bag after bag of goodies: fresh rectangular onion rolls, Russian black bread, seeded rye, fat half-sour pickles, pastrami, tongue, corned beef, potato salad, herring in wine sauce. He was like Othello back from the wars, joyous and boastful: "Look at this!" His excitement and ours in the break of routine and the frenzied unwrapping built until we were as giddy as school kids with a snow day, but my mother held back, surveying our glee from an imperious distance.

These impromptu sloppy meals did not constitute a real dinner to her, but then you could never tell what our mother would or wouldn't like. Though attractive, she was a frozen-faced woman, unsmiling, with small eyes, stiff gestures. No clothes could truly soften her thin and rigid body, make her seem less severe. And her approval was like something you chase in dreams that you both need and fear.

"We actually have an amazing deli in Ann Arbor," I said. "It's so crowded people have trouble getting in." I instantly hated the inane comments that made me sound like a Chamber of Commerce boob. What was I doing—trying to impress Simon?

He said what anyone uninterested would say in response, a polite: "Neat." And I reflected on the fact that I had never invited him or Dina to come visit me in Michigan. Likewise, they had never raised it. The silences in our family were as clear and dramatic as semaphores.

Suddenly I wanted to tell him about my new car. I held back

for a while, but I had to tell someone.

"I just bought a Grand Prix GTP," I started. "Black. Super-charged engine. Head's up display. Sun roof. Heated driver's seat. Digital instrument computer display that tells you if your oil is low, if your tires need air, doors are ajar, how many miles you can go on the gas you have left. . . ." I may have sounded like a fanatic, but I went on anyway, listing every feature I could remember, telling him how incredibly hot it was to drive the car. This got through and I could see I was seducing him into wanting leather bucket seats himself, and speed. I shared everything about the car except what the moldy salesman had said: "Young guys love this." And even though I didn't have a receding hairline or the start of a potbelly as he did, I'd been stung by realizing that guy was lumping me with himself, making us spectators of other people's pleasure. Of course that one comment cinched the deal, and maybe that's what he had in mind.

Simon and I must have had many times like this when we were growing up, with me rattling on to my little brother about the Yankees or Biology or whatever subject I was currently a self-professed expert on, while Simon basked in my relative worldliness, or I thought he did. I couldn't remember anything specific, but the rhythm of these moments felt soothing and familiar. Simon grinned when I was done now, and I shoved more knish into my mouth. I didn't feel any resentment from him, and the silence in which we continued our meal was actually companionable. At least we could share something without tension, I thought, even if it was only a ragged deli dinner.

That night, with Simon asleep on the couch, Dina still out and me in a sleeping bag on the sculptured gold carpeting nearby, I lay sleepless, recalling Old Mission. Like Simon and Dina, I had made my own private escape, as if I were a mystic seeking the pure emptiness of a desert in which to entertain visions. My last evening at Old Mission, I had walked along the cold water's edge, sliding, stumbling over a wealth of pebbles, the collar of my deep blue University of Michigan windbreaker snapping at my neck and chin. I sat for an hour on a thick shelf of slate that broke in steps into the Lake. When I finally rose to go back to my cabin for a shot of Chivas I saw something bulky and strange caught in the rocks off to my right. I got up to look more closely. A dead bloated collie, slick-furred, had somehow washed up there. I couldn't see its face and felt as much sadness as disgust. At dinner I laid a boisterous fire that ripped apart all of the darkness, trying to protect myself from the vision of that dog. I grilled a steak and prodded the coals as if that could arrange the facts for me, impart some meaning—but there was none.

I checked the next morning. Heavy rain had swept the collie back into the bay and the rocks it had been caught in were obscured by the tide.

I hadn't expected that dead dog to follow me to New York. But even with that image buzzing behind my eyelids, I still longed to go back. The words themselves—Old Mission—seemed magical, protective. It was the second time I was borrowing the cabin because up there I'd felt calm inside for the first time in years. But was it real? Like a child who's established an elaborate ritual of getting to bed to fend off nightmares—sheets so, teddy there, favorite rocks strung along a shelf in secret harmony—was I grabbing on to Old Mission to save me?

I slipped off to the kitchen in my shorts to have some juice. As I opened the fridge, Dina let herself in.

"You're up. Want some coffee?" She smiled at my near-nudity. "You look great. I guess you're still swimming, huh?" She waved vaguely at my abs, and squinted. "I don't remember the six-pack, though."

"Eight pack," I corrected, stepping back into the living room to grab my robe, rejoining her as I tightened the belt.

Dina draped her shawl-collared black blazer on the back of a chair, and fumbled with the tea kettle, almost dropping the

Nescafe jar. But there was no chance of waking Simon, who slept through anything. We sat at the small butcher block table and Dina looked tired, mouth and shoulders dropping, eyes tight.

"Did Mom say anything to you about calling me?"

"What?"

"She called me a week ago."

"Mom never called you!"

I was about to say, "She did, too!" but stopped myself. "I know. I was surprised. I didn't call back. Did she mention it to you?"

Dina sighed and shook her head. "I don't know why she would have called you about anything."

"Maybe she didn't feel good."

"So she could have told me, or Simon, or even Mrs. Gordon. Why tell you out in Michigan?"

"She could have wanted me to come in and see her." But even as I said that, it sounded unlikely.

Dina changed subjects. "It's good to get away from Serge once in a while, and that fucking French Walton family of his."

She sounded so fed up, I asked, "Why do you stay?"

"Orgasms."

"Whoa. . . ."

"You asked, babe, so I'm telling you. With Serge, I don't have to fantasize. That's never happened to me before. So when I'm in bed with him, I'm *there*. He's really good. Not passionate, but persistent. Patient. Methodical, like he's tuning a piano. But otherwise he's a jerk, *un espèce de con*."

I didn't know what to say, and we waited for the kettle to boil.

"I'm worried about Simon," she said at last, not quite looking at me.

She was always worried about Simon, always thinking about Simon. I wondered if Dina and Serge ever talked about Simon.

I knew that her boyfriends had never liked Simon, never liked her long phone calls to him, the devotion that could send her through the epic blizzard of '78 from Boston, where she was working, to New York simply because he'd called that weekend saying he had broken up with a guy and needed her. Dina didn't love Simon, it was adoration so deep I wondered if she really saw him, could separate the man from what she felt about him. She was his steady partisan, his cheerleader; nothing he did had ever seemed to shock or displease her.

We talked a bit about his bad luck with school, with women, with men, and with life. This was easy to do—like chewing over a newspaper article. He had never been happy, I concluded.

"So who is? Are you?"

I shrugged. It went deeper with Simon, but I wasn't sure how to explain that. And Dina's drunkenness was somehow affecting me, too. It seemed very clear to me that the only time I'd been truly happy was when I was in love with Valerie. Too many years ago.

"You're cute, Paul. It's been so long, I forgot." I winced at what felt like criticism for my staying away. She knew all the reasons why—all of them, didn't she? But I still felt guilty, resenting her for bringing it up even tangentially.

As the kettle started to whistle, Dina stood up without stumbling, reached for the kettle, her hand weaving, and poured hot water into her cup, groping for the spoon at its side. Her slightly acid sweat mixed with the sharp perfume of alcohol and the aroma of coffee crystals.

But something about her made me say, "You remind me of Mom." Was it the expression in her eyes?

"What?" Dina seemed puzzled, and maybe a little annoyed. We were well past the age where resembling one's parents seemed like a defeat, but it was still not the most welcome remark. Then she smiled. "She was a tough bitch, wasn't she? I guess she had to be, to survive."

38

And there it was between us: the silence, the void, the black hole in *our* universe. Our mother had survived, but neither one of us really knew what that meant to her or to us.

Dina went on. "I really don't want to go to Mom's apartment tomorrow. I don't want to start sorting her things."

"Then don't."

"God, you are so comforting. Maybe you should have become a therapist instead of a librarian." Even with her face screwed up in contempt, she looked great—imagine Botticelli's Venus in leather, Doc Martens and a sneer. But then she drooped a little, her face suddenly drained of everything, and she seemed younger, uncertain, and quite lonely.

She was appealing, but I couldn't help her, and she couldn't ask for help. We had always been a family that hardly listened, hardly broke through one another's words. We spoke to fill the gaps, I think.

As if she'd been tuning into my thoughts, she angrily blurted out, "Are you going to call Valerie while you're here or not?"

The question left me raw and ashamed, instantly thrust back into the day in my senior year of college when Dina had practically assaulted me and Valerie, demanding to know why we weren't getting married. Dina, Valerie and I had all gone out to see a movie and were back home at Mom and Dad's. I remembered sitting there on the living room couch, side-by-side, rigid, not touching, while Dina hunkered down opposite us, as fierce as a prosecuting attorney, inexplicably raving on about how perfect we were for each other, how there was ab-solutely no reason for us not to get married. She was a year younger than me, but wagged an index finger at us as if she were a wise old woman. It could have gone on for half an hour, or lasted only five minutes; however long, it made me feel utterly exposed. Valerie and I were so stunned we didn't ever discuss Dina's outburst except right afterwards. When Dina waltzed off to her room, as unconcerned as Fitzgerald's Daisy Buchanan,

I brought out a nervous, "She's crazy." Valerie, who I'd been dating for several years, shook her head, sweeping her long wavy red hair off behind her shoulders.

"Coward!" Dina said it now, just as she'd said that, and much more, all those years ago. I was older, but I felt no less exposed. I didn't even try replying.

"You know, Paul, it's not your fault you're an asshole." And then without having even sipped her instant coffee, Dina, lovely drunken tired Dina, passed out and slid—so gracefully—onto the kitchen floor.

· · · · ·

In the morning, Simon casually ate his cereal as we discussed the Will for the first time. I vaguely knew that my mother had made Simon executor, even though I was the eldest. In fact, he'd replaced whatever role she might have expected me to play in other family matters none of us liked discussing. I suppose I assumed that he had already seen her Will and could tell me what was in it, but I wasn't certain. I didn't really know anything definite, because I'd been too ashamed to ask and wasn't sure what had happened after our mother died. Each question highlighted my absence, my lack of connection.

Simon explained that he'd found her Will in the linen closet by the small master bathroom at the front of the apartment. "It wasn't hidden or anything—Mom told me once where to look. It was in a strong box, but not locked. Mostly, she kept our old report cards in there, her marriage license, investment firm statements, stuff like that, and the arrangements for, you know. . . ."

He looked down nervously and Dina gulped her coffee. Another minefield.

School reports? It seemed a strange mix of sentimentality and cold record-keeping.

"There wasn't much else I found in her apartment," Simon continued. "Papers, I mean." As if by agreement, in the last few years we'd all started calling the co-op where we'd spent most of our growing up years "Mom's apartment."

"It's your apartment now," Dina said to Simon, trying for a light tone, but her bitterness soured the words, and that fit with how haggard she looked. She was wearing yesterday's clothes and hadn't brushed her hair as carefully as usual. Yet she was still beautiful, like a model after a very long shoot.

"The apartment goes to Simon." I said it carefully, as if playing some kind of children's game with arcane rules. I felt safer making a statement.

Simon nodded. "And Dina gets the insurance."

Dina nodded almost pugnaciously as if expecting me to claim that sum for myself.

"It's $150,000," she said. "The apartment's worth much more. I don't know why the hell she divided everything this way."

Ah, yes, Dina, tallying grievances once again. Our mother was dead and we were talking about her Will—wasn't it brutal and bizarre enough without complaints?

"That's a lot of money," Dina brought out. "For Simon. And for you, especially. She left the rest to you."

There it was, then. "The rest" obviously meant "the German money," the name we gave the reparations from the West German government for my mother's imprisonment in concentration camps.

"You're joking." I could have asked to see a copy of the Will, but it would have sounded like I didn't believe or trust them.

Dina smiled, or did something with her lips that was supposed to be a smile. "Not hardly."

Simon nodded without saying anything, and I felt once again subtly accused. "It's close to a million dollars."

I must have looked incredulous, because he nodded fiercely.

"That's because Dad made her invest the money with Goldman Sachs. Over the years. . . ." he shrugged.

We all avoided each other's eyes, and breakfast continued in relative silence. I hurried to take a shower and think over the news, which left me chilled. A million dollars? I had bizarre images of Ed McMann and one of those outsized clownish Publishers' Clearinghouse checks. Where were the flowers and balloons? And why wasn't this thrilling?

Originally, our mother hadn't wanted the reparations money—it was my father who pushed her to apply as if it weren't an ordeal. Their explosions over applying for the German money had frightened us all. "You owe it to us," he kept saying, as he tried to wear down her opposition. "You owe it to the children."

Was that true? My sister Dina and I had agreed (between us) that the idea of taking money from the Germans was repulsive, and Simon was silent back then, as he was now. "Nothing!" my mother had shouted at him, eyes wide and glaring. "I don't owe anything to *anyone*."

I figured that the whole thing was just too traumatic for her, dredging up the memories she had tried to keep buried, and forcing her to consider engaging with German officials, German bureaucracy, tamer now, not grinding people into dust, but still probably heartless, cruel, efficient.

I was appalled that Dad could be so insensitive, could ignore how afraid she was, how angry. Just as I couldn't believe when my mother changed her mind and went through all the complex legal work, finding people who could swear to her identity since all her relatives were dead and her documents had been destroyed in the war, the medical examinations, going to the German Embassy or Consulate, I can't remember which. She did it all and never spent a Deutschmark of the sum unknown to me until now. When the monthly checks came in their foreign-looking greenish envelopes, she seemed ashamed, or to wish they would disappear, shuffling them quickly to the bottom of the pile of mail. Our father came to resent the German money, even though, according to Simon, he'd helped it grow. Though I never said anything, I was proud of my mother for defying him by not spending it.

That was fairly typical. We have never fitted the stereotype of Jewish families. We were anything but lively and outspoken, not a perpetual carnival of conversation at all. Dad could be social and glib, but not with us, never with us. And serious subjects just weren't on our map.

So we didn't talk about the German money, and we didn't talk about our mother's years in concentration camps. We didn't talk about anything hard.

Sitting on the edge of the tub with the leopard print shower curtain pulled back, I dried my feet and legs. The room was done in a pseudo-jungle theme, with bamboo shelving and shutters and prints of wild cats. What was that Jethro Tull song? "Bungle in the Jungle." That was Simon—a bungler. I once overheard Dad lamenting to his friends that if Simon was to drop a piece of toast it would fall buttered side down.

Because my mother had refused to spend any of her German money, and because I was usually not there when the monthly checks came, it had never seemed quite real. And so the sum had grown and burgeoned in secret—at least from us. If what Dina said was true, it was far more than I could have expected or guessed. Sometimes I'd imagined that my mother would probably cut me out of her Will because I'd cut myself off from her. But instead, she had left *me* the German money and I didn't understand. Was it a test? Was I supposed to do something with it, read it as a message?

I wondered what Dad would have said about this development, given that he had never been able to profit from the German money, and now it was mine. Would he have laughed or insulted me or said he wished he'd never badgered my mother to apply for it? No, that was impossible, because he could not have let pass that amazing opportunity to bully her.

Dad was a cruel man, thoughtless in many small ways, leaving dishes for someone else to wash, playing the TV too loud (we had to ask him to turn it down almost every night), forgetting promises, disappearing into whatever caught his interest. The kind of man I would have expected to be arrested for embezzlement—but the realm of finance was one in which he was utterly focused and clear, with everything out in the open.

Outside of that he was temperamental, accusing us of being selfish, forgetful, rude. He could barrage us with "Why didn't you—?" questions until we felt nauseous despair of ever being understood.

Treated so badly by the cousins who had adopted him, he was overly fond of getting his own way. Mother either ignored his faults or didn't care. Perhaps she even used them as evidence against him in some emotional Star Chamber.

He was like a child with us, petty, mean, but also spontaneous, bringing us treats, taking us out for surprise trips—a movie, the zoo. His aggressive good humor had always made me nervous because I thought he was acting: playing Kind Father rather than being it. Sometimes, when she was angriest, our mother called him a fool—and the English word seemed so small it overflowed with her contempt.

Was I a fool myself to worry about the German money? Could I even keep it?

Dina wanted to know the same thing, and she asked me as soon as I yielded the shower to Simon, got dressed, and returned to the kitchen for more coffee. I told her I couldn't think of an answer yet.

Dina mused, and then she seemed to see me more clearly. "Damn, Paul, you look a little green." It was said with criticism, not concern. And then she cracked up. "Like when we went on the roller coaster at Playland!"

The German Money

We'd been overstuffed adolescents at that Rockaway amusement park, having gorged on cotton candy, blintzes, and anything else we could find, and though I didn't throw up after reeling from the roller coaster, I felt like I had to for hours. Just the memory of that first vertiginous plunge was sickening, and I sat down now, my legs unsteady, and closed my eyes.

"You were so sick!" Dina rhapsodized. "You were a zombie, remember?" And then before I could yell at her to shut up, she reverted back to her new hobbyhorse. "Was Mom saving the German money for something? But what for? Why didn't she donate it or give it away?"

"She did," I said, getting my balance back. "She gave it to me."

"I admit I sometimes ask myself if you're a hopeless case, brother mine, but I don't think you'd qualify as a charity."

I let that pass.

"Simon. . . ." Dina paused dramatically.

"Simon what? Does he think he should have gotten it, because he read about the camps?"

"Well, why not? He's the one who's obsessed by all that. At least he used to be."

"You're saying it should be a reward?"

She grimaced. "Don't tell me you think a million dollars, even after taxes, is a punishment?"

"I don't know. Maybe it is."

"Whatever. But that's not why I brought up Simon. He's afraid of you."

"Me? Why?"

"He sees how you've been looking at us. Like you want to clean us up, make our lives wholesome and normal and boring."

"What? That's bullshit."

"Is it?" She pinned me with her taunting sharp eyes. "Maybe I *liked* all those years of running around and fighting with my boyfriends. Maybe it was exciting. And maybe I wanted to marry a Catholic and move to Canada. Maybe Simon's *always* going to be confused and weird. Maybe that's just who we *are*. Mom and Dad couldn't change us—do you think you can? Just because Mom's dead, that doesn't make you the head of the family or anything, money or no money. So don't think you're in charge now." It was Dina's turn to walk away, and I sat in the kitchen musing over my coffee. Was there truth in what she was saying—or just fear? And which one of us was more afraid?

• • • • •

We drove up to Inwood to take a look at the old neighborhood and our first apartment building. Call it morbid curiosity. Dina looked glamorous wrapped in a black leather car coat with the collar up, framing her face. I wondered how much luggage she had brought with her from Quebec.

"Watch out!" Dina yelled more than once as Simon almost went through a red light. Off behind us, brakes would curse and there'd be honking. The street traffic in Manhattan was bizarre, with cars weaving back and forth so quickly I kept flinching, expecting a crash, and I felt slightly ill, blasted by car exhaust with nowhere to go.

I thought of the agonizing car trips with our father, who was a better driver than anyone else on the road. "Come on, *Yankl*," he'd mutter nastily at whoever he deemed a slowpoke. "*Yankl*" was the Yiddish equivalent of "Buddy," but when he said it, it was harsh. The rest of the drivers unleashed a torrent of Yiddish scorn from Dad: "*Balvan! Flawkn! Schmendrik!*" He would curse, my mother would say "Do you have to?" and the three of us would cringe.

Fighting these memories, I kept my eyes off the road and tried focusing on the streets and buildings. And while I found some relief now and then in a glimpse of beautiful Beaux Arts stone carvings, the buildings and businesses reeled by with brutal, disorienting variety: restaurants, banks, nail salons, and newsstands giving way to liquor stores, video rentals, health food emporiums, luggage marts, cleaners, coffee shops. Flower stalls popped up again and again—as common as the reeking metal mesh garbage cans I remembered.

What had I read once about Jewish mourning customs? That Jews believed you didn't hide the reality of death by sweet and pretty flowers. I couldn't remember so many florists in the city when I'd grown up and lived there, and wondered if this efflorescence wasn't really a negative sign. Eventually I had to shut my eyes against the ceaseless, dizzying change, but as soon as I did I recalled lines a Columbia professor had intoned to us once in a seminar on the Romantics: "in my heart/There is a vigil, and these eyes but close/To look within."

Dina would have laughed, "Byron? How cheesy!" She was right, and what the hell was I remembering such tripe for now? I'd given up my Masters in English, had escaped into the far less emotional and demanding library science, and here I was being haunted by fragments of that past.

Simon and Dina were talking delightedly about changes in the city and with my eyes closed their conversation was like a radio program you could ignore. I sat back and thought about my mother. She and I had never been even casually fond of one another. She had treated me like a poor relation she'd taken in out of pity. She was polite, but fundamentally uninterested. Why leave *me* the German money?

But more immediately, why was I here? I didn't want to go back to Inwood; remembering the castle-like P.S. 98, the Fanny Farmer candy store on Broadway, the steep hill of our street, Park Terrace West, filled me with a sick sense of unreality—but I'd been outvoted. It was hard to believe this particular past, and I think perhaps we all felt that and it began to make us silly. Dina started imitating a third grade teacher we'd each had, Mrs. Zir (mockingly called Bra-Zir), sticking out her breasts and talking fruity counter-Brooklynese—the desperate accent of people unable to escape. Simon giggled, especially when Dina felt moved to chant snatches of a dirty song—"Bang, Bang, Lulu"—we'd been spanked for bawling at home. She and Simon chatted about what store had been where, driving up Broadway past Dyckman Street, the traditional border of Inwood, but it became half-hearted. Inwood was seedy and forgotten-looking, a place with no real purpose or identity for us.

When we finally pulled up in front of the huge mock-towered apartment building with its view of the Hudson and the Cloisters in Fort Tryon Park to the south, talk ceased. None of us made a move to get out.

"How about the park?" Simon suggested. "Or the playground?"

"Let's just go," I said, and we fled back down Broadway to the Upper West Side.

Driving along Broadway, we were silent in the car, perhaps haunted by images of ourselves as children, images of Mom and Dad younger, but no less miserable. Once, when I was no more than six or seven, I'd found Dad sitting in the kitchen of our Inwood apartment, a vodka bottle in one hand and a shot glass in the other. The picture was so outlandish I flinched as if I'd been smacked. And perhaps I expected to be—though Dad never punished me with his hands or even a belt—because I remember feeling afraid.

"I wish I were dead," he snarled at me, but almost as if I weren't there. I turned and ran to my room, hid in the closet among familiar-smelling clothes and toys and games.

I had never thought of raising it with him until it was too late, so the reasons for his despair that day were lost.

Finding a parking place near Mom's took half an hour, and I remembered all those nights of trying to go somewhere in the city by car and circling one block after another because whoever was driving was too stubborn to pay for a garage.

Approaching my mother's imposing building on West End Avenue, Dina unexpectedly grabbed my hand, then dropped it. I was overwhelmed by the familiar stink of the streets: a mix of car exhaust and curbs that had absorbed too many years of dogs' urine. But then I noticed the shining flecks embedded in each square patch of sidewalk, and remembered how magical they had seemed to me when I was a boy, stretching north and south as if this street could ring the world. How had I lost the sense of New York as someplace stirring, magical, rife with jarring possibilities that could make any dream seem shallow because something far better was just out of sight?

The building was a typical dark West End Avenue hulk of red-brown brick and limestone trim that badly needed sand blasting. Windows were edged with bas relief garlands and rosettes that also framed the entrance in a grim attempt at decoration.

On the way to the canopied gleaming entrance doors, I saw Dina scowl at a troop of limping dirty pigeons. There was not one that didn't have a battered or deformed leg—what a welcome.

I nodded at the uniformed doorman, who I didn't recognize. He had a comb-over so stiff he could have been wearing a piece of cardboard painted to look like hair; it gave him the air of a Senator. He smiled at Simon and Dina; it was another sign of my absence, but I was glad nobody bothered introducing me.

The lobby was as I remembered it, lavishly lined with white marble, cold as a tomb, the coffered ceiling fiendishly over-carved. And Tommy was the same elevator man as always: wizened, cheerful but remote, ageless, as short as a jockey.

"Sorry about your mother," he said to me, nodding. I nodded back. Yes, I'd been sorry about my mother for a very long time.

Upstairs, in the rectangular hallway, I felt like I was entering the lobby of a theater where every detail was painfully, unpleasantly familiar: the floor made up of hexagonal grimy white tiles, the black apartment doors and the garbage disposal door at the hallways' far end, the enormous opaque hallway windows that opened out onto an air shaft, the sagging wide staircase with its thick black railings. It was all so battered, so old, so oppressive.

But when Simon let us in, it flashed on me again that the apartment itself was one version of a New York dream: three large bedrooms, a big eat-in kitchen and servant's room my parents had used for storage, deep closets, twelve-foot ceilings, parquet floors edged with a Greek Key design, elaborate moldings, a partial view of the Hudson. I couldn't imagine living here; it struck me that day as phony, somehow, and remote.

We stood a bit awkwardly inside the front door and the scent of my mother's perfume, Chanel No. 5, assaulted me. Simon and Dina breathed in deeply too, but said nothing as we lingered by the door. It was one of those real New York fire doors, heavy, steel-cased, painted black, and bristling with locks—not like those flimsy things you see on sitcoms supposedly set in New York. Though I'd given up this city long ago, watching shows like *Friends* or *Will and Grace*—if their dopey perkiness wasn't turn-off enough—was impossible because *their* New York was unreal.

Dina took off down the dim hall to the guest bathroom; Simon sat at the foyer desk where the phone perched atop dusty address books.

The foyer was depressing: bare unpolished parquet, pale yellow-gray walls, small dented brass chandelier that looked like a carriage lamp and was over fifty years old.

I entered our old dining room, the heart of our apartment that was always brightly lit and full of food and guests.

Voluble Dad had loved company. He was constantly on the phone, clouding the air with plans, arrangements for shopping, lunch, dinner here, a party there, cards Saturday, the park Sunday, drives, walks, little visits. His hospitality had seemed rich and European to me. Friends could stay for hours, taking coffee "with something" and tea and snacks and eventually a meal to fuel the incessant conversation. It was Dad who set the tone. My mother always seemed aloof, uncomfortable, and if the conversation ever headed towards the War or anything connected to it, she would drift out of the room. It wasn't an exit as much as a disappearance; her leaving wasn't supposed to make any point.

I could tell that some of their friends thought she was haughty, acting like "a *grandamma*"—sarcastic Yiddish for "great lady." Others nodded in sympathy with the wretched memories she obviously wanted to avoid, and talked of the survivors they knew for whom the War was not over. Like the couple who had bags packed under their beds, just in case they had to flee with no warning, or the woman who filled her basement with enough canned food for an army and would never allow her children to even touch a can on the tidy alphabetized shelves.

We hadn't liked these people, these European Jews with embarrassing accents and prying eyes.

"It's as if they can tell my weight to the *ounce*," Dina had once complained. Dina was beautiful, which was appropriate for a girl, and so they evidently respected her, or at least her potential for marriage. And I was intelligent, though they thought I spent a little too much time with books.

George, a balding, shiny-cheeked custom tailor friend of Dad's, well-off, always glowing with his own success, constantly asked me about my college major in English (before I switched paths to library science) with the smarminess of someone asking a little child: "Are you a boy or a girl?"

Dina did malicious imitations of them all in her room. They were loud, crude, we thought, too satisfied with themselves, with being alive. I think we really resented how they told stories of their childhood, mentioned relatives, holidays, vacations, the Jewish sections of their cities, with an edge to their voices that showed us all that the past was real for them, everything before the War. And all that came afterwards, which was of course our world, never quite measured up.

Simon clearly puzzled our parents' friends; he was *too* interesting. They avoided staring at him so obviously it must have hurt, tried to act as if they weren't fascinated by his dark troubled life. "So young," I imagined them thinking. "So young and already no good."

We never said it, but the real problem was that my parents' friends were too Jewish and we were snobs—Dina and I, that is. We were afraid of them.

Not Simon, though. He couldn't be drawn into mockery or disdain. His silence shielded him from all of us, made him a mystery, unreachable.

Simon was our mother's favorite in a strange way; she looked at him like you'd look at a cripple, masking her pity. And Dina was closer simply for being a daughter, so why had our mother left me the German money instead of either one of them?

I sat at the dusty table, aware what an outrage this dust was in a house that had always been furiously clean thanks to my mother's obsession with hygiene. No wonder we'd all lived untidy lives in some way—who wouldn't want to break out?

With an index finger, I made random patterns in the dust layering the tabletop, puzzling over my mother's Will, over our relationship. Then I stopped, since it seemed not just as obnoxious as someone writing "Wash Me" on the trunk of a dirty car, but a desecration.

I don't think my mother ever figured out exactly how to feel about me. I knew from Dad that she'd had two miscarriages before me and maybe when I was born she found herself not as grateful to have a child as she should have been, or wanted to be. If Simon had felt not good enough for Dad, that's how I felt about my mother. Maybe I had very early sensed that none of us were entirely substantial to her, that she couldn't bring herself to care about us because she had lost everything: home, country, people, family. She never talked about the past; she had no pictures, no evidence of her life before the war—so in that way, the Nazis *had* succeeded in killing her by stealing her past.

Dina joined me suddenly, her eyes red, saying, "I'm okay."

"Anyone hungry?" Simon asked from the large dim kitchen. It was also dusty, but seemed surprisingly full of food, and some things in the refrigerator had spoiled. Dina disposed of them. The cabinets were new, a softly-stained beige wood, and the recessed lighting was also new—when had our mother redecorated, and why? I couldn't recall the kitchen needing any changes.

We ate scrambled eggs and toast made from slightly stale black bread, waiting for the coffee to brew. There was an old-fashioned Chemex coffee maker with a glass carafe that took longer than the sleeker contemporary models, but produced better coffee. Gazing at it, I pictured my mother with her strong hand around the wood collar on the carafe's neck. It was stupid, but I thought I might want her coffee maker more than anything else in the apartment.

No, that wasn't true. There was also a small Chagall lithograph Dad had given her years ago, supposedly an illustration from some French fairy tale. At its center was a haloed and horned figure, some kind of idol, and off to the right were a kneeling man and a small dog. It had always seemed a little weird to me, even more off kilter that Chagall's fiddlers and flying cows. If it were valuable, I supposed I could always have it appraised and offer to buy it from Simon.

Simon talked about the funeral some, about the small turnout, the few people who had offered to help him, help us, how he hardly heard a word of it. Someone came from Dad's accounting firm, but most of his co-workers had died of heart attacks or aneurisms so it was just a token appearance. And then my mother's neighbor Mrs. Gordon—as he'd told me before—

had been very kind to Simon. I couldn't feel Simon present in the ragged story he told, and I bleakly imagined my own funeral again. Who would come to it? The question didn't just leave me feeling empty, but childish. It was almost the pathetic reverse of that kid's revenge fantasy of imagining everyone sorry when you're dead.

Dina changed the subject. "Paul, you dating anyone?" She sounded like our mother, whose curiosity had always been mechanical; answers in general had seemed to interest her, but specific ones hadn't appeared to mean very much. Though there was always the chance of saying something she disapproved of.

I had recently broken up with Camilla, a lab tech at the University of Michigan's hospital who I'd dated for three months, until she told me she was seeing her ex-husband again. "No biggee," I told her.

Ever since Valerie, I'd always let my relationships fizzle out, avoiding arguments and confrontations, the melodramas that people indulge in to prove the vitality of their existence. I didn't need any of that. I knew I was buried alive.

What had first attracted me to Camilla when we met at Border's in Ann Arbor was her self-contained simplicity and plainness. Despite sexy wide hips and large breasts, Camilla's pale oval face and dull dark eyes—and her colorless clothes—completely extinguished any sense of her body as a passport to excitement, freedom, ease.

But Camilla had a different conception of herself. She liked setting the scene for sex like someone planning a rock garden. She lit an army of candles, chilled the wine in a gleaming cooler on the night table, set incense near the bed to helix the air with sweet pungent smoke—all in some complex geometry of the signs of passion. Then she would set the stereo to play a sound track for sex. Everything seemed so ritualized that she could have been warding off some kind of spell.

Camilla claimed to love sex, the atmosphere and aftermath

of it, voicing delight in sweat and stained sheets, the stereo still humming at dawn, smug breakfasts at all-night cafes. I suspected the fuss was the camouflage of a woman who *wanted* to be enthusiastic. "I love sleeping in the wet spot!" she'd crow. "That's because I'm a Taurus." I never challenged her raving—I didn't care enough.

Dina was waiting for an answer. I just shook my head.

"No? How come?"

"Too busy."

Dina sneered, as if I were her hapless college roommate and she were showing off a mammoth diamond engagement ring, which, in fact, was what she wore. It was seven carats and in an unbelievably ugly heirloom setting. She chewed her toast with a superior tilt of her head. "Busy? At the *library*? Don't you have all the file cards arranged by now?"

"What world are you living in? We're computerized," I said sharply, then drew back, annoyed at having been baited.

"Coffee's ready," Simon noted, rising and clattering cups.

Dina grinned triumphantly. "Then you should have plenty of time, right?"

"Coffee," Simon insisted, thrusting a mug at Dina, who took it from him with a shit-eating grin.

"I bet you haven't had a good relationship since Valerie, have you?" Dina asked cockily, her chin up as if daring me to answer. Simon startled both of us by snapping at her: "Enough."

But it wasn't enough for me. "Wait a minute! Since when did you become Dr. Joyce Brothers, huh? And why don't you hassle Simon? He goes back and forth from guys to girls. What's so great about that? You're the last person to lecture anyone about good relationships. At least I was in love with Valerie. You've never been in love with anyone but yourself."

I left my coffee in the kitchen and strode down the hall. I didn't want an apology, nor was I going to apologize myself. I just didn't want to think about Dina's brutal question about

Valerie. I spent a lot of time trying not to think about Valerie, usually right after splitting up with some far less satisfactory woman. "Val wouldn't have said that," I'd think, at least the Valerie I'd known in my twenties wouldn't have. Who she had become all these years later was a mystery I didn't want to explore, but wherever she was, I was sure her life had to be rich and satisfying—as unlike mine as possible.

Valerie and I had joked about her becoming a model or actress because of her height and long legs. People did often turn to watch her striding confidently along, her curly shoulder-length red hair bouncing, her oval freckled face slightly flushed from talking or laughing or just the breeze, her large gray-green eyes alive with observation. "Look at that!" she'd say as we walked Central Park West or through the Village, grabbing my arm, pointing at a cornice, a sign on a bus, a dog with a goofy raincoat, a pigeon pecking at a fallen hot dog, two women in leather pants suits and spiky green hair ("They must be dressed as each other," she said).

Valerie wanted me to look at everything, and I wanted to look at her.

• • • • •

The room I'd shared with Simon was large, painted sky blue, with big windows facing south. The beds, bureau, desk and bookcases were all of the same blond wood and seemed welcoming, almost tender. Standing in the doorway I remembered playing "52 Pickup" with five-year-old Simon and how I'd tricked him into demanding to go first, so he knelt down to gather the scattered cards, looking so baffled and hurt that I stormed from the room, embarrassed. Playing tricks on him—like giving him an Indian burn on his arm—wasn't fun because he didn't howl or start a fight, he just suffered.

I stepped across the threshold, looking around. The books

there were our very oldest: *Robin Hood*, Dumas, Jules Verne, Sherlock Holmes, Oz books, Lewis Carroll, *Golden Tales from the Bible*, all in shiny scratched bindings. I found the closet jammed with old shirts, worn chinos, warped boxes of writings from our first years of school, and miscellaneous mementoes that all looked like junk now. There were ancient-looking record albums, with the jackets that could have been chewed on: Peter Frampton, The Allman Brothers, David Bowie, Mott the Hoople, Jeff Beck, Traffic, Edgar Winter. I hadn't listened to them in over fifteen years and avoided all the rock stations back home even if they didn't say they played nostalgia tunes because you never knew when one might slip in. I found *Nightbirds*—the Labelle album with "Lady Marmalade"—and remembered the silver lamé skirt Val said she had worn to their famous concert at the Metropolitan Opera. God, it made her look hot. I squashed that thought.

I didn't touch anything or attempt to sort; there was no hurry because we'd decided to keep paying the maintenance fee until we were ready to move things out and put it up for sale. Simon strolled in and stretched out on his bed, hands twisting at the chenille coverlet. I knew that direct questions sometimes angered him, but I asked what was up.

"I wish I could afford to live here."

I sat on my bed. Simon rarely shared his plans or his problems with me: I heard about them from Dina. If we'd had a large extended family, Dina would have been the one arranging reunions on cruise ships, researching the family tree, making endless chatty phone calls to ensure that no one's birthday, anniversary or children's graduation was forgotten.

"Why?"

Simon shook his head.

It didn't surprise me, really. I could picture Simon living with shadows for the rest of his life, his strange disjointed past expanding, filling every room. Simon made sense here—more sense than in that tacky apartment in Forest Hills. I could never do it, since the city revolted me, and if Dina were to live here, she'd have to throw everything out in a rage of remodeling. She had houses in Montreal and Quebec City—a pied-à-terre in New York didn't seem so unreasonable and I wondered if she was thinking about buying it from him. Or would she try to make him feel guilty and want to give it away?

We were so different, I thought, yet so similar. Each one of us was haunted and unhappy. What the hell was I doing here, and in New York?

True to form, when Simon and I walked into her room there was no animosity charging the air. If Dina felt anything about what I'd said about her not loving anyone, she wouldn't be admitting it. Dina's small room, all yellows and red, was bright and likewise full of her past: photos, framed certificates, dolls, clothes, and a jumble of shoes, bold posters and broken pens. She hunted through drawers, pulling out letters and knick-knacks with a cry, shaking her head and tossing them back in. Watching her fun, I thought of having to clean up toys when we were kids. I'd be in charge; Dina would not want to stop and Simon would be lost in a private world with some unlikely-looking scrap of a toy. Mom, finding us unruly, disorganized, would say in leaden accusation, "You're not doing what I asked. You're not cooperating."

"God, Mom *hated* this!" Dina laughed, dragging dress after dress from her closet. "And this one!"

I asked her, "What does it feel like?"

"To be back?" She shrugged. "It doesn't. It's not real. I keep thinking I'll hear them talking in the kitchen or something."

Because the bedrooms were all so close together at our end of the apartment, and the dining room was for guests, Mom and Dad had talked in the kitchen at nights where we could just hear a murmur of voices like the hum of traffic down below on West End Avenue.

But if Dina remembered their late-night conversations, I remembered their discord. If they tried cooking together in the kitchen, it was chaos because they couldn't agree on anything, not even which pan to use. Simon would close the door when they argued like that, but Dina tried to intervene, fiercely reasonable in the kitchen.

That never worked because my mother ignored her and Dad would cut her down. I'd feel helpless listening to his sharp voice thick with self-importance, Mom's heavier Polish accent making whatever she said sound harsh and unrelenting.

My parents had embarrassed me, but not in a superficial way, not for being immigrants or how they spoke, it was nothing so public. Their contempt for each other at home was so blatant, at times I wished they'd at least try hiding it from *us*.

I realized that I had never seen a couple, young or old, that I admired for long, respected. It was only in movies that love and marriage seemed possible—and *that* only for two hours. I didn't know how people could be happy together. I didn't know what it looked like, and so with every new woman I'd felt I was as lost as De Soto searching for his Seven Cities of Gold. I was not as loud and dramatic as Dina, or as desperate and crushed as Simon, but I was a total failure at love—the glowing vision searched for, but always beyond reach.

"I used to wish Mom and Dad were dead, when I was little," Dina said with a smile.

"I just feel blank," I said.

Dina eyed me for a very long time. I turned away. Maybe I blushed.

Dina shrugged. "I don't know why, but I never thought it would be like this. All this stuff still here. I can't deal with Mom's room. Let's start some other time, okay?"

Yet none of us seemed willing to leave the apartment and we drifted back out to the living room that seemed cavernous with its large windows framed in sheer white curtains, and the fireplace empty and dark. The twin mauve couches were new, as was the square slab-like marble coffee table between them. Very Pottery Barn, and not what I would have pictured my mother buying.

"Where's the Chagall?" I said. There was an oval mirror in the corner to the left of the fireplace where the lithograph had always hung.

"Oh, Mom said she got tired of it, she gave it away or sold it or something. After Dad got really sick." Dina was as offhand as if it had been merely a calendar. "You know she never liked it. I don't know why Dad even bought it for her. She hated Chagall."

That was right. More than once I'd heard her call his work "Jewish dreck." Was that why I had liked the strange lithograph? Contemplating its absence, I felt as sulky as a slow-running child clutching change while the ice cream truck drives away down the street.

"When did Mom get all this new stuff?" I settled onto one of the pillowy couches. At least not all of the room had changed: the walls were still as thickly covered in family photographs as those English manors are slathered with paintings, one hanging above another. They'd almost all been taken by Dad and framed and hung by him.

There we were, Dina, Simon, and I, from infancy on, at every possible turning point through adulthood, and for all the endless smiles and posing, the effect wasn't warm, but calculating—the way a collector shows off prize specimens. Yet Mom had never expressed much pride to us about being our mother.

I glanced away quickly from the photographs of me and Valerie, and some of Valerie herself, stung to see them hanging there like historical plaques marking a disastrous battle. I had expunged her from my life, or tried, even burning her letters and cards some years back. But my mother hadn't been fueled by any similar impulse. She had approved of Valerie. How did I know? Because she never squinted at her suspiciously, the way she did at other girlfriends of mine or Simon's, and because she'd shared recipes with Val. This, I knew, was serious between women.

It was also a bit revolting to be confronted with all these moments plucked from my past: my first tooth, 6th grade graduation, me at my first lifeguard job in high school. The walls seemed to snarl and grab at me, telling me there was no escape from the past, from my past. No escape.

A little while ago, back at Old Mission, I'd been staring up at the universe, lost in vastness, and now my universe was reduced to this clamor of memories.

From West End Avenue, from Riverside Drive and the West Side Highway came the maddening storm of trucks and cars, shifting and braking and crushing the air. The noise stunned me. Planes droned by overhead, buses whined and groaned, bizarrely clangorous car alarms went off sporadically and conversations echoed up from the street with fierce intimacy. Listening to it was like being trapped underwater in a tidal pool where the current beat and beat at the rocks.

Dina waved a hand at the furniture. "This stuff? Oh, last year, I think."

Simon wandered around the room, straightening frames, while Dina sat down right opposite me and fixed me now with her hard, tired eyes.

"You know, Paul, to tell you the truth. . . ." She hesitated, and I cringed a little at that introduction. I knew from having been born and raised here that New Yorkers were always prefacing something unpleasant with that phrase. It was as much a theme song as "New York, New York." I should know, I used to say it.

Dina crossed her long slim legs, smoothed down the skirt of her dress.

Simon was staring out a window, or maybe just turning his back on both of us and not really looking anywhere but away.

Dina uncharacteristically cracked her pretty knuckles and started over. "Paul, I'm very disturbed about the German money." She looked as grim as someone planning revenge.

"No kidding," I said. "I remember what we said years ago, how it was disgusting to take that money."

"No." She waved that away. "I don't mean the idea of it. Not at all. Why shouldn't the Germans pay for what they did? Look at Israel—the whole country took money from Germany. But that's not my point." And here she leaned forward as if to emphasize her sincerity and concern. "It's just not fair," she said, voice unsteady. "Why do you deserve to be singled out—because you're the eldest? That doesn't make any sense."

"Maybe not to you. It must have been sensible for Mom."

"So now you're an expert on what Mom thought, what she wanted?" She leaned back, arms crossed, face flushed, surveying me coldly, not so much looking like Mom, but holding herself as if Mom's spirit had taken her over. I wished Simon were right next to me to see this, but he was sitting off behind Dina, on one of the window seats, arms wrapped around his legs, curled up, almost, as if he wanted to shut us out. Would he start humming loudly next? Sitting there in his dark blue turtleneck and chinos he looked like a cross between ads for The Gap and Prozac.

I felt myself flushing like Dina, too, as my uncertainty and confusion about the German money was temporarily eclipsed by my anger at her. If I had the money right then and there in cash I would have pelted her with wads of bills to make her shut up.

"You should split it among the three of us, Paul. Everything should be split up: the co-op, the insurance, the German money. Everything."

"That's okay with me," Simon called from his perch, but he ducked his head down when I glared at him, and he mumbled something that sounded apologetic.

"See?" Dina said. "That's two of us who agree!"

"But Mom didn't. Mom didn't agree with you. She made her own decision. I don't know what it means, but she did. Why can't you accept that? Why do you have to control things and have it all go *your* way?"

"Fuck you! Since when did you care about what Mom wanted? What anyone wants!"

"Why are you defending Mom when she was so cruel to you?"

"Bullshit. Mom loved me!"

Before I could even process that bizarre remark, Dina surged on: "You didn't even come to my wedding. Mom came—and the church service didn't bother her at all. She thought it was beautiful! So what the hell was your problem?"

"It wasn't that. I wrote you—"

"Yes, you *wrote* me. Thanks a lot. A goddamned letter like I was some stranger!" With harsh mimicry, she quoted, 'Dear Dina: You know how hard it is for me to be around family.' What the hell are we? The Borgias? The Manson Family? What's so terrible about us that's kept you away from us, away from home for years?"

She knew, but despite that, I said, "This isn't my home."

Dina grinned evilly. "See what I mean? You went to Michigan!" She made it sound like a profound betrayal.

"Well, what about you? You had to take that editing job in *Boston*? There weren't enough publishers in New York? And then you married a Québécois and moved to Canada? Gimme a break, Dina. How much time have *you* been spending in New York lately?"

Simon glanced up as if waiting to see what Dina would say, but she didn't bother answering the charges. In fact, she didn't say anything for a few moments, perhaps surprised I'd strike back just as personally as she had attacked. Or just that I hadn't folded.

In the silence Simon coughed and said to me, "You could give the German money away to a Jewish charity, completely, and we could split everything else. Then we wouldn't have anything to argue about. . . ."

Dina rounded on Simon and hissed, "I will *never* talk to you again!" If she weren't so serious, I would have laughed at her childishness.

"Face it, Dina—you don't get to decide what happens to the German money. *I* do."

But even as I said it, the claim sounded like sheer bravado. This was no simple inheritance, and I felt overwhelmed by it.

"You don't care about Mom or us or anything. You've become a fucking robot," Dina sneered.

"And you've become a selfish, willful, spoiled bitch," I said coolly, testing the words as I brought them out, finding their weight comfortable. Then I upped the ante. "Let me take that back. You were always a bitch. No wonder you and Serge aren't getting along."

Dina sprang up, and I was sure she was going to lean across the marble table and spit in my face, but the doorbell rang and we all turned to it and then stared at one another like figures in a French farce wondering where to hide.

The doorbell rang again, and the three of us trailed dutifully but unwillingly to the door with Dina muttering, "Who the hell. . . ?" There was some awkwardness as Dina and Simon both moved to open it, then danced around each other, while I tried to hang back but ended up tripping over the tall terra cotta umbrella stand. I caught it and kept it from breaking and spilling out its contents as Simon opened the door.

"Mrs. Gordon," he said, with a slight lift in his voice.

On the black rubber welcome mat stood a diminutive, round-faced woman with tiny dark eyes and a lush head of silvery hair, leaning on one of those metal canes whose base splayed out into four little feet. Pear-shaped and dressed in pink sneakers and a green track suit, she was somewhere in her late seventies, I guessed. Her hands were gloved in wrinkles. She smiled genially at Dina and Simon, revealing refrigerator-white teeth (or dentures), then more broadly at me, piping out a cheerful, throaty, "You must be Paul."

She grinned knowingly as if guessing that I expected her to add the sickening cliché of "I've heard so much about you." What she did say was, "You're back with family," her dark eyes slightly hooded. She must have read the tension between us and her remark was so quietly mordant that I couldn't help laughing. Dina and Simon looked startled, then annoyed. Dina threw off something about calling her husband and she disappeared into the kitchen, the door swinging after her.

"The elevator boy told me you were in the apartment. Will you be around a little while?" Mrs. Gordon asked us. Simon and I glanced at each other and nodded. "Good," she said. "I'll bring up something sweet." She shrugged again. "What can I tell you? I'm old, I bake." And she turned and made her slow way to the heavily grilled door of the elevator, half-turning to wave a little goodbye. In her crinkly green track suit she looked like a figure on a St. Patrick's Day Parade float.

After the door swung shut, I asked Simon how well he knew her. From the kitchen I could hear Dina's low querulous voice.

"She moved in last year. I think somebody left her the apartment? I don't remember what her story is, but she hung out with Mom."

Hanging out wasn't a term I associated with my mother, but from her accent, Mrs. Gordon was probably Polish or Russian, and a Holocaust survivor, no doubt.

Before we could seat ourselves back in the living room, Dina burst from the kitchen, grabbed her car coat and announced, "I'm going back to Queens. I'll get a cab." She waggled what was apparently a set of Simon's keys and stalked out to the door without even saying goodbye or "Seeya."

The heavy door was flung open, then Dina called back to us, "Don't take anything while I'm gone." The door slammed behind her with the rattling thud I remembered.

"*Take* anything?" I asked Simon. "She's unbelievable!"

I'd been about to ask the expert how much a cab would be from the Upper West Side to Forest Hills, but then I realized it was meaningless to Dina, since Serge's family owned a chain of Lexus dealerships in Quebec, and she had stopped worrying about money when they got married. Worrying about *her* money, anyway, or what she already had.

The apartment seemed very quiet without her, painfully so, and Simon and I sat opposite each other a little stiffly. We could have been passengers bumped from the same flight, having run through our litany of complaints and finding ourselves with nothing else in common. Face to face with him, alone, I wished once again that I were back in Michigan. I even wished I were fucking Camille with her whole sexual sound-and-light show.

Quietly, Simon said, "Dina's not really a bitch. She's not as bad as you said."

I nodded, more to keep him talking than because I agreed. Dina had always been an angry woman—our mother's death wasn't likely to mellow her out.

"It's just. . . ."

"Serge?" I asked.

"Yeah." It didn't trouble me, for a number of reasons, the chief one being that I'd missed Dina's wedding and so it had never registered with me as having taken place. I'd stayed in Michigan because I couldn't stand the idea of plunging back into my family at the worst possible time. There's something nakedly primitive and tribal about weddings, no matter how you cover them up with flowers and ceremony—the group is in control and individuals don't seem to matter much except for what they contribute. Going to her wedding, I would have not just felt lonely, but almost ridiculous in that atmosphere. And my being single and in a poorly paid, unremarkable profession would have felt like a badge of shame.

Dina resented my not coming, as I probably would have in her place, so I had only met her husband once. A few years after her wedding, I'd been in New York for a conference, and Simon had mentioned in one of his rare phone calls that Serge and Dina were doing a theater weekend. As it happened, my time there overlapped with theirs, but I'm not sure why I thought it might be worth trying to reconnect with Dina and at least meet her husband. We rendezvous'd for drinks at their hotel, the Plaza Athenée, which Serge probably liked as much because he could speak French to the staff as for its *"luxe, calme et volupté."* In the dark glittering lounge, I had felt underdressed, even shabby, as I often did back in the city of my birth after having moved to Michigan. It wasn't only my clothes, I think, but my attitude. I felt oppressed and unhappy there, unable to screen out the tumult. It wore me down.

Dapper, Bijan-suited Serge was conceited from his mop of curly brown hair to the fingertips of his flawlessly-manicured big hands. Dark and lean, he had the theatrical, paper-thin magnetism of a Las Vegas illusionist. "You're the librarian," he'd said with fake enthusiasm as he pumped my hand hello. His hearty manner was probably a sign that he wanted me to believe he didn't hold any grudges against me for not coming to the wedding. Despite the grin, he clearly felt that my profession was just a step above homelessness. "You must love books," he added, making conversation as if he were gearing up to sell me a car.

My mother didn't know I was in New York at the conference, and I'd asked Dina and Simon not to tell her. It seemed a sign of liberation to me to return and not feel obliged to "check in." So of course that was the first thing Serge mentioned. "It's terrible you're not seeing your mother," he said, legs crossed at the knees, his accent as decorative as the monogram on his French cuffs. "Family is very important. Me, I have three brothers and three sisters and I would die without my family."

He would die without his Patek Philippe, I thought, watching Lauren Bacall sweep past us into the lobby.

Dina was very quiet that evening, very beautiful, giving Serge her version of the Nancy Reagan devoted look, and adjusting her black taffeta skirts with her left hand so that the diamond bracelet she wore caught as much expensive light as possible. She ignored the celebrities, and her graceful silence seemed an obvious comment on my poorly explained absence from her wedding. I kept trying to steer the conversation to anything neutral, but Serge wouldn't give up, rhapsodizing about his own "*Maman.*" I suppose he switched to French because English couldn't capture the depth of his feeling at that point or the subtlety of the concept.

If I disliked him for his own sake, I disliked him even more when Dina later informed me that she was giving up her editing job, not because it would have meant splitting her time between Boston and Quebec, but because it wasn't "dignified," according to Serge and his family. She should be at home, supervising the household, or out shopping and lunching with suitable friends. When I asked her if she wasn't outraged, Dina simply said, "You wouldn't understand," without explaining any more. She didn't have to. It was the kind of dismissive remark a parent might make to someone without children.

"Serge is handsome, anyway," Simon observed now, as if that made a difference. He even smiled a little, encouraging me to join him in his assessment.

"Sure—Dina always dated good-looking men, who else would she marry? But she has better taste in clothes than in men. That hasn't changed."

Simon nodded and then silence swept up around us again. It was like one of those disorienting moments when you're driving on a highway at night and suddenly there aren't any cars behind you and the rearview mirror is completely dark.

I had escaped New York for many reasons, but this was one of them: awkward silences. I preferred the distance and the safety of an answering machine that screened my calls. When I'd moved to Michigan, I had assumed that it was far enough away for me to avoid unexpected or even planned visits from family, and I'd been right. As if they were super heroes, and the Hudson liquid Kryptonite, they'd all stayed on the other side and left me alone.

And of course there was Simon himself. His whole confusing history of trouble had always frightened me a little. When Dina spoke about Simon, she often quoted the French saying: To know all is to forgive all.

But I hadn't felt that about my brother. I knew too much and his disasters unnerved me. If he had been my older brother, his screw-ups would have been satisfying. I would've benefited from them if only by unspoken comparison: calm and reliable, not scandal-plagued. But Simon was four years younger, young enough to embarrass me growing up. I never talked about him to friends because he was a puzzle, because I couldn't savor his defeats.

I couldn't be comfortable with his college drug-dealing, his bad trips, his disco slut girlfriends, his poor grades, his gambling, his flings with guys, his car wrecks, his brief marriage to a girl he didn't know and apparently didn't like—all the irregularities that left him untouched somehow, as if his life were a medieval painting with him innocent, saint-like at the center, plagued by writhing demons. Was there something cruel in an innocence that survived so much chaos?

Simon and I both sighed now. Luckily, the bell rang again.

"Mrs. Gordon," we said together, with intense relief.

I stood up but let Simon get the door. Mrs. Gordon made her careful way through the dining room alone. I couldn't tell how much she needed the cane, perhaps because though she was slow, she moved steadily across the parquet floors. I came around the couch to help her settle next to me, but she shook her head, "It's for getting up that I'll need a lift. This way, it's another story, I have gravity helping me." And she laughed. "Simon is putting the goodies on a plate." She sat down and looked even smaller with the thick, high back and arms of the couch looming around her. One hand held onto the cane.

Simon returned with a plate full of rugelach and some napkins, set them down on the table. "I'm tired," he said. "I'm going to take a nap, okay?"

"Sure."

"So," Mrs. Gordon beamed up at me, turning half towards me. "You're alone—at my mercy!"

I smiled back because she was not much over five feet tall, even with her slightly bouffanted hair. And because she was so relaxed. Watching her, I could feel how tight my neck and shoulders were, and even that my jaw was clenched. After being hemmed in by Dina and Simon, it was a relief to be talking to someone who wasn't family, someone with whom I had no history whatsoever.

I reached for a napkin and one of the rugelach.

"Honey apricot," she said, watching me carefully for my reaction. She didn't have to worry—it was sweetly succulent, a perfect mix of crunchy and soft.

"Wow. This is great."

"Have some more," she said. "Please. I make them with real butter and real sugar. Not so good for my heart, but your heart can take it. It's young, still." She reminded me a little of Dad and Mom's old friends, most of whom had died or moved away, but she seemed much softer, less like a conceited fortune teller who knew the unimagined dangers you were headed for, but was reluctant to share the future. Unless I was the one who was different. And then I thought, Was Mrs. Gordon right? *Was* my heart still young?

"Have some more," she said.

"Why? Do you think I'm too skinny?"

Pursing her lips, she let out a gently dismissive, "Noooo. . . . Are you kidding? You look fine. You're what us Litvaks called a *yaht mit beyner*: a well-built man. But just now, you look like you could use something sweet."

"You're right." I ate under her approving eyes. She wasn't quite old enough to be my grandmother, but I felt as relaxed with her as if she were.

If I had expected her to say something about my mother's death or my being back with family or anything like that, I was wrong. She asked, "So, how do you like New York these days? Nice and clean, huh?"

"It's still New York. It's hard to get used to."

"You're, what, in Ann Arbor, in Michigan?" She pronounced it almost like "Mitchigan." "Tell me something—they have phones there? Indoor plumbing? They got the wolves under control?" When I hesitated, she said, "Don't mind me, I'm a kibitzer."

"I'm pretty tired."

"I can see that." She nodded. "New York is tiring. But that's why I like it. After my husband died, *olav ha-shalom*, the house was too big, and the stairs, they bothered me. We were on a little hill, you know, with too many steps down to the street. But I didn't want to move to Florida or Arizona. Too many *alter kock-ers*. I'm alive, I want to see life. Here in New York is life, here is all kinds of people. You got your museums, movies, restaurants, the kind of thing they don't know from, any place they got an early bird special, or—" she shuddered "—a club house. Believe me, I know, I've been to plenty of them on visits. So I moved to New York."

"Where did you move from?"

"Northern New Jersey—near Denton? You know where that is? Not far from the George Washington Bridge. It's not much, highways and hills. But my husband, he had a diner. The Olympic," she said proudly. "He was a Greek man. I baked most of the desserts, you know, the favorites: cheesecake, lemon meringue pie, chocolate cake, coconut cream pie. We had a good life." She shrugged and held out her hands. "What can I tell you? I still have a good life—only different."

It could have been the sugar, but I felt more energetic than I had since arriving. Here she was, an elderly widow with a cane, and yet she was jaunty and optimistic. What right did I have to be so gloomy? And hadn't I just inherited more money than I'd ever dreamed of having? But as soon as the question occurred to me, I felt tight with distress.

"What's wrong?" she asked, frowning. "Do you need some water?"

If I'd said yes, I bet she would have limped to the kitchen to get it for me.

"Did my mother ever talk to you about the War?" With that question, I felt as exposed and relieved as a patient sharing a secret torment with a psychiatrist, knowing he wouldn't be judged, and hoping, ultimately, for comfort.

The light in Mrs. Gordon's face dimmed a little. She shook her head and let out another pursed-lipped "Noooo. . . . Your mother, she was very private. And besides, it wasn't long we know each other, so—"

"I don't think she ever talked about it, not even to my father."

"And that's so bad? You know what's wrong with Americans? I'll tell you. They talk too much, they tell any stranger on the street about their divorce, their daughter having an abortion, anything, doesn't matter how terrible. *Gevalt*! They don't even need to be on TV to have a big mouth. People on the bus will talk your ear off. Nothing's personal. Nothing's private. By me, sometimes not to talk is better than talking too much."

She meant well, but having made the plunge, I couldn't pull

back. "But it's always been a mystery. What happened to her? What was it like in the camps for her?"

Mrs. Gordon shook her head and stamped her cane for emphasis. "You think if she told you it wouldn't still be a mystery? I can say I was in the Vilno ghetto, and the camp at Riga, and evacuated to Stutthoff when the Russians moved west and how there was a big storm on the Baltic and we thought for sure we was gonna die and talk to you for days, and believe me, still you wouldn't understand. Nobody who wasn't there can understand what happened to me. Nobody."

She wasn't bitter or accusatory. If anything, she was calm, saddened as much for me as herself.

"Does it bother you that I brought it up?"

She leaned forward. "It's okay. Your mother's dead, and you turn to someone. It's not the same among your family. But I have some advice. If I were you, I would try to live my own life. It's too late—"

"Too late for what?"

She smiled, ran a hand across her forehead. "Who knows? I forgot what I was going to say. It happens. And now, I need your help."

I put a hand under her elbow while she used the cane to heave herself up. She felt almost weightless to me, so her short struggle was surprising. I accompanied her slow progress to the door. "I hope I see you again," she said. "But that's just because I'm an old lady, and you can get sentimental about someone you just met since you never know how much time you have left! But for you, believe me, the best thing is you go home as soon as you can."

I let her out into the hall. It didn't seem possible to close such a heavy door without making a lot of noise; still, I tried, not wanting to wake Simon up.

The street noise hadn't diminished, but the light was changing in the apartment and somehow it felt like a quieter place than it had before. I wandered around, opening kitchen cabinets, taking out souvenir mugs I'd long forgotten. I stepped into the dining room and opened the built-in china cupboards, fiddled with some of the crystal. I tried recalling when I'd last eaten there, but couldn't picture myself or any of us. With Mom's death, somehow the memories had drained from these rooms like one of those movies where the color is slowly leached out of a scene at the very end. It all looked rather stark, and I felt as if I were noticing the crown molding in this room for the first time, and the window frames, and the slightly bowed and peeling latticed window seat whose real purpose was to cover the radiator.

Simon wandered into the dining room, rubbing his eyes. "There's some coffee left," he yawned.

We drank it in the kitchen, while we demolished the plate of rugelach one-by-one. I filled him in on my conversation with Mrs. Gordon, less to share it than to go over it for myself.

"She's right," he said. "I agree with her. What's the point of trying to figure stuff out now?"

"I need things to make sense." After all, I'd learned to tie my shoes very early, my mother had said; I'd been fond of lining up my childhood books by size; my bureau drawers were always neat. Adding to the portrait, my grades had always been high, I had never caused trouble or talked back—in school or at home—never really wanted to. Mom had sometimes recounted this evidence of stability not to praise me but to condemn Dina or Simon in one of their more difficult periods.

"You want sense? In this family?" He leaned back in his chair, with as much ease as if the apartment had truly always belonged to him. Mom used to hate when he'd do that—"Stop! You'll tip over." And her warning almost sounded like the hope that he would, to prove her right. But he never had. That was too simple a mistake for Simon to make.

Yet sitting there in the kitchen opposite him, without Dina

around, I felt surprisingly more relaxed than even a few hours ago. Was it Mrs. Gordon? I had few elderly neighbors or colleagues, and wasn't used to spending any time with a woman her age, who was old enough to be my mother, but actually felt grandmotherly.

"I love this place." Simon observed, his eyes unfocused. "It's different with Mom gone."

I knew exactly what he meant. Our mother was like the mean principal lurking around the corner in your elementary school ready to pounce on your slightest misdemeanor. Enjoying her space without her presence, or the threat of her return, was a luxury we'd never really had.

I asked him, "Weren't you surprised Mom left me the German money?"

"I was surprised it's so much. That's the big surprise." Unlike Dina, there was no rancor in his voice when he mentioned the money. "Are you going to quit your job?'

"Why?"

"That's what I would do. Live abroad. Spend it all." And his smile was lascivious.

"Then what?"

He shrugged. "Who cares. At least you could say you went someplace." Suddenly he sat up sharply—"Hey, Paul, remember Mom and Dad's obnoxious friend George? Remember when he and his wife went to Greece on vacation? Do you remember what he said when they got back?"

I couldn't recall any details.

In a passable Yiddish accent, Simon snarled, "'For this we had to go all the way to Greece? I could have visited the South Bronx to see *tzebrechener shteyner.*' Broken stones! Can you believe it? It's almost as bad as that Jewish joke about the couple that takes a trip around the world and says they didn't like it. 'Next year we'll go someplace else.'"

Simon chortled, more animated than ever, and with all this

talk of travel, I oddly found myself remembering a conversation with Dina when we were both in college. She had proudly announced, "Simon wants to go to Maine."

"Maine?" I asked. "What for?"

"To be free," she breathed, as triumphant as if Simon had discovered something essential about life. I don't know what he'd read that had inspired this sudden vision, but I suppose he wanted to be free of himself, without knowing that was a prison no one escaped from.

I hadn't had the news about my mother's bequest long enough for any volcanic fantasies to explode inside of me. But I fixed on Simon's question. If I were to quit my job, I didn't think I'd suffer. I wouldn't miss my colleagues, or the University of Michigan, or even the students. Helping them with their research was the only enjoyable aspect of my job now, which had otherwise become a mindless occupation that paid the bills. It said nothing about who I was or what I wanted in life. Had it ever?

"I'm not going to work tomorrow," Simon told me now. "Do they have good pizza in Ann Arbor? We can order pizza and stay here tonight, if you want."

I didn't really want to leave, either, so I said, "Sure." Simon hunted in a kitchen drawer through takeout menus, found one for a restaurant he said he remembered and made the call. Then he phoned Dina at his place to say we were staying over. From what he said, it sounded as if she was glad to have more time to herself. And the way his face and stance softened reminded me once again of the intimacy of their relationship. He and Dina talked for what seemed like a long time, as if they'd been separated for weeks, not just hours, before I got on.

"How's Simon?" was her first question when Simon handed me the phone. Of course, it wasn't enough to talk to him, she needed confirmation from me. That's what I was good for.

"Alive," I said.

"Oh, God! Dad used to say that to his friends, remember, when they asked how he was?" Dina repeated Dad's joking answer in Yiddish, something he must have picked up from his parents: "*Ich lebt*." It usually came complete with a Jewish shrug.

I said nothing, feeling a little dizzy at the vivid picture of my father, and the telephone line hissed. We always avoided talking about Dad.

"When I got back," Dina hurried, "Serge called. He was so sweet. He misses me. He apologized for our fight. Listening to him was *sensas!*" she said in the French slang she had picked up from Serge: sensational.

Mentioning her fight with Serge—whose subject Dina hadn't disclosed—did not naturally lead to discussing our argument. No, that would have been too logical, and too out of the ordinary. Even my mother's death hadn't changed that for Dina and me. The rest of our brief conversation was just as superficial; we could have been distant relatives making a yearly holiday call.

Death had not brought us closer, unless you considered being angrier at each other an improved kind of intimacy.

When I hung up, I said to Simon, "She wants you to count the silver."

He knew I was kidding, but admitted, "That was dumb of her, before."

We turned on the radio, which my mother had always kept tuned to the wonderful classical station WQXR. One of Beethoven's earlier piano concertos was playing, and the bold, bright music echoed through the apartment as we went around turning on lights.

When the pizza came, I noticed Simon checking out the lanky, dark-eyed delivery boy, who seemed Korean. Simon probably tipped him too much, but I didn't know if that was on purpose, or because he wasn't paying enough attention to his wallet. Though it didn't seem to me that the delivery boy had noticed, I felt a little embarrassed to be witnessing this, and also curious.

Simon dug out Diet Coke from the pantry and we served ourselves in the kitchen, me at the table, Simon standing with his back to the stainless steel sink. I decided to take another plunge, and asked, "What's it like for you? Being bisexual? What's it mean?" I had never asked him this before.

Saving some cheese that was about to drip off the slice he was holding, he stared off to the side as if looking for a cue card, then bit off the end of his pizza slice, chewing slowly. I did the same, savoring the thin crust and the sharpness of taste that I missed back in Ann Arbor. It's a great college town with lots of cultural attractions, but it's a town for all the pretensions, and New York pizza is New York pizza. Of course there could have been an element of nostalgia in the comparison because when I thought of pizza I was instantly back in a crowded, raucous pizza shop on Broadway, after school, having a slice with friends and enjoying the freedom of being between two worlds of restriction: school and home.

"Did you ever read *Women in Love*?" Simon finally asked, done chewing.

"Sure. In college."

"There's a scene where one of the characters is in a rowboat with someone else and they're at opposite ends and perfectly balanced. I think he calls it 'star equilibrium.' It's his ideal."

"Do you want that . . . with a man, or with a woman? Both?"

"I just want it. I always have."

"Is it possible?"

"You tell me." He smiled. "You're the smart one."

What did *I* want? Simon's quotation made me think of desolate lines I'd read in a poem by W. S. Merwin about the stars looking to *us* for guidance if we ever figured out what we needed.

"But isn't that what you had with Val?" Simon asked, eyes watchful, perhaps expecting me to shout at him as I had in the past, once or twice, when he'd brought her up.

It had always felt like prying before, but now, with all the death we'd been confronted by, Valerie seemed dead, too. At least talking to Simon she did.

"I don't know. I don't know what I had with her. Maybe we had too much." I felt my throat drying out and I slugged back some more Coke. I wasn't sure how much more I wanted to know about Simon's personal life, but I'd never been this comfortable around him, and I was honestly curious, so I continued.

"How is it different?" I asked. "With one sex versus the other?"

"I don't do it with a whole sex, I do it with a person. Everybody's different."

"I know that, but there has to be more."

He closed his eyes as if calling a scene forth. Eyelids shut, he said, "Okay, with a man, at least for me, you never know for sure where you're going, what you're going to do. It could be anything." He didn't elaborate. "With a woman, no matter where we start, I always look forward to sliding inside of her—"

"Yeah, that's it. But doing it with a guy?" I shook my head. "I can't see that. Isn't it a little gross? All that hair. . . ."

He sighed, fixing me with his striking eyes. "Come on, Paul, don't you admire other guys' bodies at the gym when you're working out, or other men in the pool?"

"Of course. Sort of. When somebody's in good shape, it's like we're on the same team. It makes me feel good."

"Okay. So why is it so hard to imagine going further?" He struggled to put it together for me. "Like you're not just looking at him, and you, I don't know, mentally note he's buffed or whatever, but when you look, you don't want to stop. It's not just that you, like, admire his shoulders, but you're all the way into really checking out the different parts of his deltoids, the tie-in with his biceps, the vascularity when he raises his arm. You haven't touched him, but somehow he's touched you. And you want to run your hands across the muscles, feel their shape, how hard they are, smell his skin. See?"

"I got it. Taking inventory. That's how I feel checking out a woman."

"There you go." He nodded decisively. "I get drawn to women, I get drawn to men. It's different, but it's the same. That's just my nature," he added, peering at me to see if I got the joke.

Of course I did, and I laughed because it was a line Dad often used that was his way of shrugging off complaints or criticism.

Simon seemed pleased, but then his face changed and he looked almost wary. "And before you ask, yes, I've been tested and I'm negative. I never have unsafe sex."

I hesitated. "I guess *I* do. I hate using condoms."

Simon frowned. "And your girlfriends let you?"

"Most of the time. Hey, I'm a Menkus man, right? I make 'em an offer they can't refuse." And we basked in our father's remembered crudeness for a while. He'd often said, "Women have always liked the men in the Menkus family, because we're *big*."

Talking about sex made me think again of how much Camilla had enjoyed nibbling on my foreskin. I'd been her first uncut lover. "Like a curtain going up," she sometimes said, watching it slowly retract while blood rushed pleasingly on stage. I liked entering her only partway before I was fully hard, so that she could feel my foreskin still bunched near the head of my cock, and then teasing her as I slid back and forth. An all-natural tickler that made her growl, "You bastard."

It was a natural question, so I asked Simon, "Do your lovers like that you're not cut?"

Simon frowned. "But I am."

"What!"

"I got circumcised a long time ago. I never told anyone, not even Dina."

"By a—" I hunted for the word.

Simon supplied it: "A mohel? No. It was at the health center at Tucson. Janet kept getting infections and this doctor said it was because I wasn't 'clean.'"

Simon never mentioned his ex-wife. They'd met in Tucson at the University when he was twenty-three and finishing college for the third time.

I started to object because we'd been well-educated as kids on washing ourselves "down there," but he said, "I wasn't clean enough. I was so coked up those days I didn't really think it through. But now I'm glad, because it makes me feel like I'm really Jewish. It hurt—for weeks. And I was swollen up like a bat. A baseball bat, I mean."

"Did it help Janet?"

"It seemed to."

It felt very disorienting to think that Simon was—even haphazardly—closer to our father and all the Jewish men in our family than I was. I definitely wanted to change the subject, so I asked him where he would go if he had the German money.

No hesitation. "Thailand, for sure."

"To see the temples?"

"No. For the sex."

I tried again. "You said there wasn't much stuff in Mom's strong box—did you look anywhere else?"

"Not really."

We spent the evening searching the apartment for something, anything that might provide a clue to Mom's bequest. But there was no diary among all her bills and receipts, no letters, not even any check stubs with her papers. Even more puzzling, we couldn't find any independent record of the German money besides the bank books and statements from her investment firm. There was no safe in the house, no key to a safety deposit box, nothing. It was not at all what I expected. Shouldn't there have been a welter of personal papers? I thought of my own desk drawers at home crammed with letters and notes and memos—all of it filed and labeled.

"It's like she never even applied for the German money," I said. Never applied, never visited the German consulate, never had witnesses testify to her identity, never had a single argument with Dad about it. Did that mean she hated it?

But the money was waiting, untouched, growing year-by-year.

We had agreed to sleep over there that night, so Simon took Dina's room. We found plenty of linens, and washing up, we could almost have been twenty years younger getting ready for bed.

I could hear Simon's rattling gloppy snoring soon after he hit the sheets, but if I slept in my old bed, it was restlessly, and I woke thinking I'd heard my mother's voice. Dazed, wondering for a moment if I were in Michigan, my whole body pulsing with alarm, it began to sink in that I'd only been dreaming, or perhaps I was half-wakefully drifting in and out of memories of Mom's own nightmares.

For years, perhaps until I was in high school, my mother would cry out in her sleep unexpectedly, sometimes as often as twice a month: wordless heavy animal anguish. In the violated darkness of our apartment, Dina, Simon and I would cluster together in the hallway, waiting for more, but of course Dad would wake and hold her and the next day he'd look at us in warning not to mention the nightmare whose terrible shape we never learned.

And sometimes the terror hit my mother when she was napping and one of us had to shake her where she slept in the living room. The first time I remembered doing it, I was only ten or so, reading *Bomba the Jungle Boy* in my room when her cry seemed to slap the book from my hand and shove me to my feet. I crept down the hall to find her on her back on the gold-threaded overstuffed red couch. Her face was foreign, squeezed, and she moaned in some language I didn't recognize. Beginning to cry, I poked at her leg and she rolled onto her side away from me. I ran to the bathroom to wash and wash my hands as if they were stained by her fear.

Now I was fully awake, and I began to think that what had really woken me up was the unfamiliar smell of cigarette smoke. I pulled on shorts and followed its bite out to Dina's dark silent bedroom. The door was open.

"I smoke when I can't sleep," came Simon's invitation. I walked to his bed and sat at the end. He was clearly nude under the sheets; he had a slim, naturally lean body, molded by exercise, and was more handsome than I could ever be, I thought, unless it was just that the darkness was kinder to him. You couldn't see the anxiousness that creased the corners of his eyes and made his mouth rigid. Simon offered me a cigarette, but I passed because I usually smoke only when I've been drinking Seven and Sevens heavily. Simon moved an enormous, green alabaster ashtray onto the bed between us, and sat up more, the sheets dipping a little. I wonder if Dina ever commented on his abs, too.

"Janet gave me that," he said, pointing at the ashtray with his free hand. "Sometimes I miss her. Do you miss Val?"

The question was rhetorical. He wanted me to say yes, to share his loneliness. That wasn't hard to do, so I said "Yes." But missing Valerie hardly described what giving her up had meant to me. Somehow I'd imagined, in part anyway, that moving on, moving to Michigan, trying to forget her, was being mature, was like a private ceremonial, a rite of passage. But all I'd achieved was a change of scene. I had the scarification (inside), but I had not been transformed. *De*formed was more like it.

"Janet made me laugh. No one else did. But that wasn't enough."

"So what is?"

"Fuck if I know." He sounded stronger, less tentative, as if the night freed him. "Remember bisexuality was cool in the 70s, and now it's cool again? People think you have twice as much fun. But for me, it means I have twice as much chance of screwing up a relationship. And I do."

I suddenly felt torn by an urge to pull back, to retreat to my room, to force myself asleep. This wasn't us, this wasn't how we talked to each other. Instead, I told him about breaking up with Camilla, partly because I had to tell someone, partly because I didn't want to think about Valerie any more.

Simon took it all in as intently as a jury. "If the sex was phony, and you weren't that crazy about her," he asked at the end of my recital, "Why'd you date her?"

"Fuck if I know," I echoed. "Why date anybody?"

"God, we are so messed up, you and me and Dina. What's going to happen to us?" he asked, the way you'd wonder if a plane was about to crash.

I thought of Old Mission.

Simon put out his cigarette, shifted Janet's ashtray to the floor.

"Paul? Stay till I fall back asleep?"

I took his hand and squeezed it. He smiled, squeezed back and let mine go, closing those strangely troubled eyes. I was glad his eyes were closed because I must have been blushing and there was enough light leaking through the window shades from outside to see that. To my surprise, I found myself feeling that I loved him, loved my gentle soft confusing brother, betrayed by his own complexities. I sat there peacefully while he withdrew into a safer world, his body twitching, then shifting into sleep, possessed by darkness now and ease.

Heading back to my bed, I tried to remember when I'd held anyone's hand and it meant so much.

I slept late and found Simon making blueberry pancakes in

the kitchen. "I found some old sweats of mine, and shoes, so I went running," he said. "And I picked up some groceries on the way back."

I ate several helpings, but before I could head off to shower, Simon told me that he'd called Dina in Queens. "I think it's time to go see Dad," he murmured after a while. And I knew there was no way to avoid it. I was too exhausted to try. We had spent the last couple days together deliberately not talking about Dad, delaying this moment.

"We'll pick up Dina in Queens and all go out there together," Simon explained, clearly having worked this out in advance. I didn't argue. There was no point.

Nine years before, we had all urged my mother to put Dad in a nursing home—Simon and Dina on the spot, me over the phone. A series of strokes had brought on something very like Alzheimer's called multi-infarct dementia, which I had never heard of before. I had seen an x-ray showing that his brain was dotted with tiny white spots, little explosions. "All those dots," my mother kept repeating, as if amazed that something so innocuous-looking had destroyed his mind.

At first he was just very forgetful, leaving his keys in the car, or inside the apartment. Then it got worse. He couldn't remember dates, and kept circling them on newspapers and in magazines, as if throwing out one tiny lifeline after another. He was a dapper dresser before, with a fondness for expensive ties and cufflinks, but now he was putting on striped shirts and hound's tooth trousers, forgetting to wear a belt or tie his shoes. He'd watch television shows he'd never been able to stomach before, like nature specials, shaking his head, "It's very sad, very sad."

No doctor, no test offered hope. Trying to help, Simon read every article and book he could find about senile dementia, but learned nothing that gave himself or Mom comfort. I tried reading about it, too, but gave up a few pages into one book that said having a loved one with dementia was like attending a funeral every day of your life. I threw the paperback out; after all, hadn't we grown up in a house consumed by mourning? I couldn't embrace any more of it; I was not that strong.

My mother was, or thought she was. "I will take care of him," she insisted. And she could, for a while. Bathing him, feeding and dressing him, talking to him constantly as if to lure him back out of the fog that had descended on him so quickly. It was agonizing to hear her talk and talk to our father, pulling only puzzled and strange comments out of him. He wondered where he was, or why she was bothering him. I knew some kind of crisis was coming when he stopped speaking English, and only answered us, when he did, in Yiddish.

It made my Mother furious, for some reason; maybe she took it personally, took it as an escape from her, because they had always spoken English between them. Yiddish was something my Dad used—as an adult—fairly clumsily. But his parents had spoken it at home, and now the words of his childhood were back. I had learned some and could understand what he was saying. But Mom was so angry it seemed to block her ears.

Given his deterioration, Mom had taken legal steps to reorganize their estate so that he could not inherit if she died before he did, but that was the only time Simon or Dina had mentioned Mom's Will to me.

I learned most of this secondhand because visiting was too painful. Dina would call me with desolate announcements: "He told Mom he hates her." Or: "He keeps asking me who 'that woman' is in the apartment." Or: "He's incontinent most of the time." And we would reflect on the horror in silence. I remembered once in 4th grade losing control of my bowels just as I got home, and my mother's appalled orders, sending me right to the bathroom to strip and bathe. I kept apologizing to her all day but she grimly ignored me, washing out my soiled shorts in the bathroom sink as angrily as someone chiseling an inscription off a memorial stone. And this kind of horrible discomfort and humiliation was happening to her again—but with her husband? Unimaginable.

Driving out from Manhattan on the Long Island Expressway to see Dad that day, I remembered how much, and how oddly, our Mother disliked Long Island, disliked anything even vaguely rural. "So many trees," she sniffed, like a dowager forced to step around a homeless man blocking her limo. It had always struck me as some kind of affectation whose meaning I couldn't understand. Now it hurt to think of all those trees and neither of our parents able to see—or at least appreciate them.

The nursing home, an hour and a half from the Upper West Side, was good for its kind, or good enough, with a high staff-to-patient ratio. The shell of my father was washed every day, shaved, his hair and nails kept trimmed and neat. Simon and Dina had both assured me that he never got bed sores, and that there had been enough money set aside for his care. The unspoken part was that he would probably not live too much longer, given the congestive heart failure that was creeping up on him.

The place was called Cedars of Lebanon, which struck me as grotesque. Nobody here was tall and strong any more; they were all shrinking, shriveling into themselves.

But the place was disgustingly cheerful, so intent on making you feel serene it gave me a headache just to walk down a corridor. The walls and carpeting everywhere were rose-pink or pale blue. Impressionist prints or posters, cheerfully matted and framed, hung in all the public areas, with lights over them to give the appearance of discrimination and taste. The overhead lights were unmercifully bright, and nothing hid the hopelessness, the sense of this building being just a giant refuse bin, where elderly men and women had been dumped because there was no place else for them. The few previous times I'd been there, I'd thought of suicide, vowing I would never let myself end up so helpless, so sick, so devoid of life. And in Michigan, every time I used to read about another one of Dr. Jack Kevorkian's exploits,

I felt grateful knowing that I wouldn't have to suffer from a lingering, crippling disease if I didn't want to.

My first time at the nursing home, a brisk, chunky, gap-toothed nurse had cheerily given me a small tour that was worthy of Hamlet's gravedigger. When we passed a stairwell, she assured me that patients were encouraged to use the elevator. "Because if they fall—" she shrugged "—they could be there for hours." She said "they" with an utter lack of compassion—as if she were a lab assistant talking about her mice. And in the brief look at the library with freestanding metal shelving, she leaned to me and said confidentially, "Don't bother donating books. They don't read much, unless it's large type."

My father's floor was the worst because it was for those who were completely incapable of activities of any sort. Here people were beyond communication, beyond being entertained, though the TVs kept playing. The ancient-looking patients slumped in wheel chairs, had to be fed (several at a time). The sprightly signs, the decorated bulletin boards in the rooms, the briskly cheerful nurses (cheerful that they could move and speak, I often thought)—none of it could camouflage the macabre gargoyles propped up in the wheelchairs and "gerry" chairs that kept them from hurting themselves. Every visitor whose eyes met mine had the same ravaged look: "This could be you."

In the car, Simon had told me he visited as often as he could, to check on Dad's care, and to keep him well-dressed, because we all had images in our head of badly dressed nursing home patients—people mis-buttoned, carelessly wearing plaids and stripes together, or colors that clashed, as if it didn't matter anymore. It mattered to Simon and Dina, and to me. Simon kept him supplied with the Old Spice cologne he had loved, and he smelled remarkably fresh, but still looked like a caricature of himself: wasted and gray. The life had gone out of him, taking his color, his animation, his gusto. This was not my father. This was a shadow, a ghost.

The German Money

I felt the same dread approaching him that I'd felt before, even though it had been over seven years since I'd last seen him, as if he was merely a doorway to some horrible universe of oblivion and pain, and I could succumb if I got too close. Dina also held herself back, talking to him stiffly, talking to watery, pouchy eyes that registered nothing. Dad's face had lost its comic edge and looked swollen, melted, drained. His skin had turned splotchy and what was left of his hair looked like the lines children scrawl on a pencil drawing of a head. No wonder we never talked about him.

Simon surprised me. He was gentle and loving with Dad, feeding him patiently when he visited, speaking in a reassuring undertone as if to tame a violent horse. Simon had gone to see him almost every day that my mother couldn't.

Thankfully, Dad had just been fed and we circled around him in the sunny alcove where he was marooned in his gerry chair, rigid, unseeing. The air around us was stifling—with some kind of flowery disinfectant covering up a staleness, an emptiness, and the weirdly metallic scent of old people's shit.

"Dad," I said, as if I had to speak first because I was the eldest. "It's me, Paul. Mom is dead. It was a heart attack."

Nothing. Not a flicker of change in either of us.

Simon knelt by my father's chair. "*Tatinkeh*," he said in Yiddish. "*Di mameh is geshtorbn*." Daddy—Mom's dead. He turned to me and said, "I've told him already. I keep telling him."

"When did you start speaking Yiddish?" Dina asked. I tried not to look surprised that this was something Simon hadn't shared with her.

Not turning around, Simon muttered defensively, "Since he got sick. It's just to him." Dina shook her head and grimaced as if Simon had taken up water-skiing in an attempt to reach Dad. To me, Simon's gesture seemed quixotic, and brave. It would have hurt me to try.

Dad blinked, and Simon took one of his stiff hands. The

twisted spotty fingers did not stir. I think Dad once had powerful, thick-fingered, manly hands. But I wasn't sure.

"This would kill him," I said to Dina, as I had before, in person and over the phone.

"I know."

We both were referring to his former vigor, how shocked he'd be if the impossible could happen and he was able to see what he had become. But in truth, I think that each time one of us said over the last nine years, "This would kill him," it was like a tiny hopeful prayer. Please. Soon.

Simon and I waited down in the lobby while Dina found a Ladies room. I tried not to look around because the expressions of visitors were too wrenching, too naked.

"Are you ever glad they're both dead, now?" Simon asked so quietly that at first it didn't register. When the question sunk in, I must've looked surprised, because Simon sounded a little sharp: "Well, Dad *is* dead, isn't he? That's how I think of him. What's there—that's not really Dad anymore."

"But you come here so often—you said so. You spend all that time feeding him. You talk to him."

"It's like a memorial." He blinked rapidly a few times. "Well, *are* you glad?"

"Why?"

"It doesn't hurt so much."

"What doesn't?"

"Hating them."

· · · · ·

We took another silent drive back to Simon's apartment, only this time heading west. These were the boundaries of my time in New York: death and vacancy, first the cemetery in New Jersey and now another kind of death park. No, that wasn't right—there was more here in the city, there was the German money. But that still seemed polluted to me, almost dangerous. My mother had never spent any of it. Had she been unwilling? Afraid? Had she feared it would somehow harm her, that there was a trap involved? Perhaps it was her superstitiousness, because she knocked on wood more than anyone I'd ever known. Maybe she felt cursed to have survived, or haunted.

One time years ago, I'd woken up near dawn to take a leak and heard something strange when I opened the bedroom door, a shushing down the hallway. I edged out and peered down it in the darkness, trying to see and hear better. It came from the foyer. Creeping forward, I began to make out a figure seated at the foyer desk—Mom. Gradually I saw that she was alone. She was talking to herself, whispering in Polish or Yiddish, I couldn't tell. "*Shaydim*," was one of the words I seemed to hear. I'd heard the word among Mom and Dad's friends. It meant ghosts, malicious spirits. I couldn't make out the rest of what she said; I was too scared to call to her or move. The whispering stopped, I retreated into my room. I don't know if she'd noticed me or how long it lasted. I don't know why she sat there and said anything at all. I lay there thinking I'd seen something unbearably intimate, wishing Simon had woken up, too, so that I wasn't alone. *Shaydim*. Or was it *shame*?

Just then, we rolled over a pothole so big the jarring made me feel like a college running back getting one of those hard tackles Keith Jackson called a "slobber knocker." I glanced back at Dina and over at Simon, but neither one registered having just been shaken and not stirred. That was life in New York—perpetually screening out whatever was unpleasant, I supposed, until you were numb. But who was I kidding? Wasn't I numb out in Michigan?

No, not completely. I could feel the sunsets, I could enjoy the plangent murmur of mourning doves. I wasn't dead. Not yet, anyway.

Dina sat quietly in the back seat until her tiny cell phone

rang and she started speaking very low in French. I knew it was Serge, but couldn't make out much of what she was saying. But I did hear the word "*Allemagne*" more than once. German. She must have been talking to her husband about the German money. Why?

When I turned to look at her, her head was down but she was grinning so triumphantly, I wondered if the call was part of some game she was playing, and she had won this round.

When she was done talking to Serge, she said, "Serge wants me home. I'll leave today. I can come down some other time and go through things at Mom's."

She was so ebullient I wanted to shoot her down and ask her why she was no longer worried about Simon or me stealing anything of our mother's, but I kept quiet. Simon didn't respond to her announcement or even look back at her, but even from the side I could tell he looked surprised, maybe even hurt. Surely he thought he was support enough.

We bounced along home. People in Michigan complain about the state of the streets and highways; well, they should all try a day driving in New York and they'd feel much better. I couldn't believe the ravaged-looking roads that wouldn't have been out of place in a disaster movie, the kind I couldn't watch because the screaming, fleeing crowds always made me think of my mother in the War.

Dina was back on the phone, pulling out her date book and dialing Air Canada. By the time we drove up to Simon's, she had already switched her flight and Simon drove her to La Guardia as soon as she was packed. She kissed me goodbye as if embarrassed to do it, and I wondered if she was running from the threat of closeness between us, the possibility of change.

Opening a can of soup for lunch, I imagined Simon and Dina at the airport, fond, affectionate, even holding hands. Sometimes people took them for twins as much for their connection as any resemblance. Picturing them there I felt once again excluded and alone. When Simon returned from the airport, I told him I might want to stay at Mom's apartment a day or two before heading back to Michigan. Staying in Simon's strange garish apartment that seemed like a disguise whose purpose I couldn't guess was even less comfortable after having had a real bed and real space at my mother's.

Simon looked relieved. Maybe he wasn't used to having guests, or maybe he wanted to bring someone home he didn't want me to meet. I'm not sure it mattered why. I packed up methodically, as if arming myself for a hazardous encounter. Simon had mentioned the subways once or twice as a possibility since I'd brought just one bag, but I countered with stories about people being pushed off the platforms.

"That doesn't happen anymore," he said, as if it were out of fashion. But the very idea of it terrified me. Growing up, I'd worried—as everyone else did—about crime in the subway, but murder hadn't been a threat back then. You could be mugged, or more likely grossed out, coming down a reeking staircase to find a bum laid out, his head haloed by vomit, or watch rats scrabble on the greasy tracks late at night. I understood from articles I'd read and reports Dina and Simon both had given me that the subways were safer, cleaner, more salubrious—but they still weren't my idea of a sane place to be.

When I was ready, I called my boss at the library and got a few more days of bereavement leave. It was easy, almost too easy. When I'd announced my mother was dead, I'd been annoyed by the melodramatically sympathetic looks of my co-workers. They all seemed to be acting out an image of commiseration they felt uncomfortable with. Perhaps they were embarrassed at the demands they thought my situation made on them, since I kept my private life so private. All I'd wanted was silence, and to get away.

Simon gave me his extra set of keys for Mom's apartment. We surveyed each other at his door, moving together awkwardly for a quick hug, acting as clumsily embarrassed as tyros at a dance studio.

I headed downstairs and hailed a cab, nervously aware that I could probably afford it now. I refused all invitations to chat with the driver, who was Haitian judging from his name. He tried roping me into complaints about Congress and Jennifer Lopez and people who let dogs lick their faces. The last topic seemed to make him angriest and I did wonder if there was some ethnic basis for his disgust, but kept my eyes closed while he ranted. I tipped him well out of relief to be leaving his cab.

And then there I was, in my mother's apartment, surrounded by the air she had been breathing just a little while ago. Temporarily, at least, I was in complete possession—but of what? There was furniture here and clothing and dishes and books and porcelain figurines and jewelry and framed Modernist prints, but what did any of that have to do with Mom, or Dad?

In the kitchen I opened the liquor cabinet, which, as always was sparsely stocked with inexpensive vodka and some sweet liqueurs like Cherry Heering. As kids we'd thought it was somehow made from herrings, even though we'd tasted the cough-syrupy drink and knew the difference. Dad had loved Cherry Heering, smacking his lips before he even filled his heavy shot glass, and to tease us he always called it "Cheery Herring." For him, though, liquor was all basically "schnapps" the way they say Southerners refer to all pop as cokes.

There were some unopened gift boxes in the cabinet and in one of them I found a bottle of Seagram's. My mother had liked Seven-Up and always kept a lot in the pantry, so I was soon seated with a very stiff drink back in the living room.

Questions jostled me. My father had been an only child; his parents died long before he met my mother. Now I would never be able to ask her what he'd said about them, what they were like. And Mom—what must it have been like to come to America after having survived the Nazis and see some home-grown fascists rise up with McCarthy? I knew that she had met Dad in Paris after the War, but couldn't recall if either one had ever told me how exactly they'd crossed paths, what they'd said, how they'd looked at each other. I know there were some photographs of them, Mom with a 40s pile of hair, Dad in a rumpled Army uniform, but there was nothing written on the back to tell us where the picture had been taken, or by whom. I'd never asked Dad about serving in the Army, and he had never volunteered anything. I'd been afraid of his reminiscences, knowing that they would invariably lead to meeting Mom, eliding from his War to hers.

But all that was lost. I'd been so desperate to escape New York and the past, but now I felt starved for it. And I would be hungry in a way that could never be satisfied.

I had lost, through my parents, access to my own past. Looking through photo albums, finding old souvenir postcards, I would not be able to plumb their memories, to hear the stories. I hadn't just lost a chance to retrieve details of vacations, illnesses, scholastic triumphs—I had lost the very details themselves. My mother's death, Dad's disappearance into a virtual death, had taken huge chunks of my life. I wasn't just alone, I was diminished, reduced.

No wonder people had kids. How else could they feel they weren't being erased with each passing year? But I had never met a woman I'd want to have kids with, except Valerie.

I made myself a third drink. Hell, I wasn't going anywhere—in more ways than one—so what did it matter? In the silent kitchen, the ice cubes and gurgling pop bottle sounded admonishingly loud, but there was no one to snap at.

Back in the living room, I let myself be drawn to the wall of framed photographs, seeking out the ones featuring Val. She was tall, slim-hipped, with full and pointed breasts, and had never considered herself beautiful, perhaps because her freckled face was too angular, her nose too thin. But when she smiled it seemed to ignite her deep red hair and hazel eyes. Angel Eyes, I called them, after the song on Roxy Music's comeback album that we had listened to so much in freshman year at Columbia.

I downed half of my drink, perched myself on the window seat Simon had claimed yesterday when Dina and I were arguing, gazing out at the thick oily-looking dark water of the Hudson, shot through with lights from the myriad buildings across the river forming an uneven crenellation of the Palisades. The beams reaching out across the water struck me as sad, incomplete almost. New Yorkers had traditionally mocked "Jersey," but growing up, I had studied the stretches of green and brown between buildings and factories that made the state across the river seem so different. I'd wondered what it would be like to live somewhere that wasn't completely covered in concrete and asphalt, but the stretch of Jersey shoreline I could see just seemed to be aping Manhattan. Had Val and I gone there once on a double date with Dina and someone I couldn't place, off to a jungle theme park? I tried to track down the memory, only glimpsing Val in a halter top, insubstantial sandals, and thin cotton skirt buttoned down the front. And I remembered getting sunburned. Nothing more came back, but it made me happy to have just that.

When I told my parents Val and I had broken up after five years, Dad was disappointed and angry. "Idiot! Valerie's a prize. What are you, *meshugah*?" But my mother had put it far more painfully because she was so much more precise: "You will never meet a girl more kind." Whether that was a threat, a curse or simply an observation, it was just like my mother to zero in on something irreplaceable. Lots of girls were pretty, smart, talented, affectionate, even Jewish—but kind? It was an old-fashioned, uncommon quality.

Time and my own fuck-ups had proven my mother absolutely correct. I raised my glass to a picture of Valerie off behind me. A group shot of both families on the July 4th when we'd had a party and used our bit of river view here to the fullest, watching boats on the Hudson. Even my mother was smiling in that shot, standing stiffly behind us kids with Dad and Val's parents as if they were somehow ushering us into the future. And she was smiling in another photo with Valerie and some little girl I didn't recognize.

Dina and Simon had both been fond of Valerie, and the reverse was true. I'd liked her parents and they had approved of me. A love fest all around, right? But I had jumped off the carousel, unwilling to snatch the brass ring.

"You'll regret it," Dina had said, her voice harsh and vengeful, as if I had somehow offended her personally, and she was weaving a spell that would guarantee my unhappiness. That wasn't necessary—I'd done enough to fulfill her prophecy. Simon's reaction was more befuddled, but that may have been due to whatever drugs he was into at the time. I suppose if he had broken his sibylline silence, he would have made some dire predictions, too. Maybe he held back because he knew how right Dina was.

Angel Eyes. I found myself humming that song. I trailed back to Simon's and my old bedroom to see if I had left the Roxy Music album behind with the others when I'd moved from New York and taken mostly cassettes because they were so much easier to pack. Rifling through the junk on the closet floor, I found "Manifesto" and their "Siren" album too with probably their best-known song: *Love is a Drug.* Oh yes, Bryan Ferry got that one right.

Simon's battered secondhand Bang & Olufsen turntable was still on our particle board wall unit, and I slipped "Manifesto" on without bothering to do all the needle and record cleaning he'd performed with surprisingly ritual exactness.

I lay back on my bed listening to the music I had discovered with Valerie, trying to place where exactly we'd been the first time we heard the song and I thought of her. "That's you," I'd said with a grin of discovery, marveling at Bryan Ferry's brilliance. "Angel Eyes."

I did see Valerie blushing and turning away, but snuggling against me, beautiful eyes averted. She had said quietly, "Okay."

Listening to the album, eyes closed, I was surprised to remember very different music. One winter when we'd had tickets to Seiji Ozawa and the Boston Symphony Orchestra at Avery Fisher Hall, I'd waited for her on the chilly plaza of Lincoln Center, imagining every possible urban disaster when she was late because she was scrupulous about being on time, and then spotting her, finally, striding along in her black, fur-collared Dr. Zhivago coat, grinning at me because she'd instantly read my panic and my relief. How we'd hugged there and I'd wanted the weight of her body in my arms to know she was all right, I was all right. Inside, when she took off her coat, men and even women stared. She looked like a model, and much older, in a new long-sleeved lilac woolen sheath that was tight at the bust, violet hose and high heels, and the antique garnet necklace I'd given her for her twenty-first birthday. That evening, every note in the coppery, golden hall sang of her and I felt dumbstruck by how stunning she was. Valerie was like an undiscovered country that an explorer has dreamed of and knows with ineffable intimacy: strange and blessedly familiar at the same time. I had trouble speaking during the intermission and we just held hands and enjoyed the beautifully-dressed crowd. Did we drink something? The first half had been a Mozart Piano Concerto played by Alicia della Rocha, and it didn't prepare me for the emotional juggernaut of Tchaikovsky's Pathétique after the intermission. I knew the piece from the radio, but didn't even own a recording and had never heard it performed. As the symphony progressed and the music worked on me like a storm about to tear the roof off a Florida home, I felt seized by a desire to ask Val to marry me, but not just to lean over and whisper it. No,

The German Money

I wanted to clutch her slim wrist, drag her along our row, up the aisle and out onto that open gleaming plaza, to whirl her around in my arms and shout it as if life were a musical: Marry me! Marry Me!

So why hadn't I?

Bryan Ferry was singing the sad, romantic *Dance Away*. I sat up, concentrating, trying to stay back there with those moments in which my life could have changed completely. But all I really connected to was the rapture, the rush, not the inhibition. No, that wasn't true. Even lying there alone in my mother's apartment, I was still unwilling to face everything that had separated me from Valerie. Or more honestly, everything I had let separate us. Valerie's parents were Holocaust survivors just like my mother, and the idea of marrying her had at times felt like tying myself to the Holocaust for the rest of my life: it would shadow everything I did and said if I married a child of survivors. How could I ever escape those images of death in the ghettoes and the camps, the sense of being hunted, a victim? It sickened me.

Unlike my mother, Valerie's parents talked about their trials openly. And Valerie had grown up not feeling imprisoned or bludgeoned by their past, but energized. She had never run from it, she'd faced it squarely and turned it into a strength, a source of inspiration. "I'm proud of them for coming to America and starting a new life. Think what that took!"

Valerie spoke a language at such times that wasn't just alien, it was threatening. Marrying her, I would be struggling to learn it, or block it out. I'd hear the endless rattle of chains that bound me to the bombings, the ghettos, the camps, the smoke stacks, the torture, the bulldozed piles of corpses. Her very ability to talk about it all so honestly, so freely, sometimes seemed obscene, and even made me angry because I felt like such a failure, such a coward.

That's what sent me fleeing from her, from New York. That's what stopped me dead the night we listened to the Pathétique.

Marry her, and I would never be free of my mother's horrible past.

Valerie and I had been so close, I'm sure she picked up my unexpressed excitement the night of the concert, my inner frenzy. Perhaps she'd even known exactly what had seized me. Like lots of couples, we often completed each other's sentences or would find one of us raising a topic the other had been thinking about only moments before.

After the concert, when we were having drinks at O'Neal's across the street, she looked very sad, almost rueful, even when we spotted idols of hers: Peter Maartins sprawled at a table with other noisy dancers, and Edward Gorey, sitting by himself, face as wittily enigmatic as his drawings. I couldn't remember what we'd talked about. But it had been a little chilly, and she kept her coat on for a few minutes, looking, I thought, as if she were undecided about staying. I did tentatively ask her about her mood, but all she said was "The Tchaikovsky hit me pretty hard."

The memory faded and once again, I was thinking that my mother was dead. I said it to myself a few times, feeling around it the way you check a sore tooth with your tongue. And so was Dad, really. I had no parents any more. I was an orphan, wasn't I? And as I drank my Seven and Seven, I mulled over what that meant. I felt as cut adrift as the astronaut floating out into cold, heartless space in *2001: A Space Odyssey*—from them, from myself.

The doorbell rang a few times before the sound penetrated. I shut off the stereo and stumbled out to the foyer. Before I could put my eye to the peephole, I heard "Paul? It's me."

I fumbled with the locks, wrenched open the door and gaped. It was Valerie, looking exactly as she had back in college, with her red hair curling to the shoulders of a tightly-belted beige trench coat, her flushed face making the freckles on her nose and cheeks brighter. How many times had we stood at this doorway, kissing hello? And hadn't she had a coat just like that years ago?

"I hope you're going to make yourself another Seven and Seven," she said softly. I stepped back and let her in. "Because I think you need it." As she passed me and I let the door clang shut, I thought, No, she wasn't the same. Her stance, her walk, had more authority, and she seemed taller.

Like a zombie, I helped her out of her coat and hung it up.

"Your perfume," I said.

"Angel."

"What?"

"It's Angel. That's the name."

She stood there smiling at me, taking me in. And now I was back with my first impression of her looking the same as when we were in college: she wore black clogs, wide-legged black velvet trousers and a long-collared white silk blouse and black v-neck sweater. I'd always loved her in black.

"Your clothes. . . ."

She looked down at herself, then shrugged. "I know, the Seventies are in. Again. Why not?"

I beckoned her into the kitchen and she sat down at the table, crossing her long legs and glancing around fondly, casually. I made us both drinks as I often had years ago, being careful not to yank open the freezer for the ice cubes or drop either the bottles or the glasses. After a date we liked sitting here because it was almost in the middle of the apartment so if we talked, we'd feel somewhat private.

This was utterly wonderful, utterly bizarre.

"But how—?"

"Simon called to tell me you were on your way over here, I had some free time, so I thought, why not?"

"Simon." At least it hadn't been Dina. Then I thought: *She wanted to see me.*

"You're in touch with Simon?"

"Now and then."

I nodded, uncertain what that meant or how I felt.

"It's been a long time," Valerie said carefully. "I'm so sorry about your Mom. It was a shock."

"Thanks." I wasn't sure what else to say. I nodded, standing away from her with my back to the sink. "How did you know what I was drinking?"

"When you drink Seven and Seven's, you always get this little crease in your forehead, there, between your eyebrows." She pointed and I flinched as if I could feel her finger pressing into the spot. In bed years ago, after sex, she had liked to trace a line around my eyes, never explaining what, if anything, it meant to her, though I'd asked many times.

"I think it's always there now. I'm getting old."

"Right. And you're obviously falling apart," she said, sipping her drink, eyeing me over the rim of her glass.

"You sure it wasn't Dina who told you I was here?"

She looked startled and crossed her arms. "No, not at all. Why would she? I would still come by here anyway, now and then, to visit Mrs. Gordon. She would have told me about you if Simon didn't."

"Wait a minute. How do you know *her*?"

"I'm doing another book. This one is going to be based on interviews with survivors. Your Mom didn't want to be in it, but she told me about Mrs. Gordon downstairs, and. . . ."

Now I sat heavily at the table and thunked my glass down. "Wait! Back it up. *Another* book?"

"You didn't read my memoir?" Val looked disappointed. "Didn't you hear about it?"

I shook my head.

"Five years ago? *Shadows of the Holocaust*?"

The title told me everything. Even if I'd known about it, I would have avoided it.

"I was on NPR's *Fresh Air*," she sad proudly. "It went into four printings and I stopped having to freelance so much. Paul, you're a librarian, how could you miss it?"

"Hey—there are over 150 books published in America every day. And even though I read *Publisher's Weekly*, it's not cover-to-cover. It's easy to miss things. Besides, the Holocaust isn't my area." I stopped. How many excuses was that? Too many.

She shrugged lightly. She looked even better than when we were dating; was it success that had made her more attractive? She was forty-one now, a year younger than me.

I tried to reconnect. "It must have been exciting, getting published."

She didn't reject the overture. "You're not kidding. I mean I'd been doing book reviews for Jewish magazines and newspapers for years. . . ."

I tried not to look as if I hadn't known that either.

"But this was bigger. It was amazing! Knopf sent me on tour after it started to do well. You know how publishers are—they were apprehensive because of the subject, but they were wrong. I had a limo and driver in each city, it made me feel like I was a celebrity. Wait a minute—the book was reviewed in the *New York Times*, and you missed that, too?"

Spoken like a born New Yorker, for whom the *Times* was the touchstone of reality.

But we were not going to make any progress here while she acted like a neglected author and I felt foolish. "I guess I did. And Dina never mentioned your book. Simon didn't either, not that we talk much. I'm sorry."

She still looked hurt, and even doubtful, though I wasn't sure if she was more annoyed at my family for keeping it back, or at me.

"Val, I'm just a librarian."

She smiled as indulgently as if I'd explained the oversight was due to a decade of undersea exploration with Jacques Cousteau. "Okay, Zizi, I forgive you."

I cracked up at my old nickname. We'd read Cocteau's *The Infernal Machine* in French Drama at Columbia, and in it, Queen Jocasta's nickname for the priest Tirésias is "Zizi." It was French slang for penis and sometimes, with warm mockery, that's what Val had called me. I was surprised she'd use it now, and must have looked as fawningly dumb as a spaniel getting its belly rubbed.

Valerie looked slightly uncomfortable, as if embarrassed she had used the nickname, but I found myself madly grateful to whatever force in the universe had brought me to my mother's apartment tonight. And glad Simon and Dina weren't here to witness this reunion and turn it into a production, Dina by raving, Simon by dramatic silences. "Don't screw this up!" I commanded myself though I had no idea what that meant.

"How are your folks?" I asked.

"They retired."

"Florida?"

"What else? They have a condo in Boca and spend the winter there. They kept their apartment here. They still like to go to shows, and they want to see me and—" She broke off, as if mildly abashed at her volubility.

"You know, I was just listening to Roxy Music before you rang the bell. Don't you think that's weird?"

"No. I listen to them all the time."

"You can stand it?" Her face changed, and I hurried on, "I mean—Well, isn't it painful?"

She said, "Duh. . . . That was more than fifteen years ago."

"That" meant our love affair and our breakup. It was an oddly vague way to put it, but maybe vagueness suited us best right now. I tried to shift gear. "You said you were shocked when my Mom died. . . .?"

She'd known me well enough to have heard the question I wasn't asking. She uncrossed her legs and leaned back in her chair. "I never stopped seeing her after you left New York, Paul.

I liked her. I know she was hard on you, but I liked her. I came over every few weeks and we had lunch. Sometimes we went shopping together. Clothes shopping. And I always figured she was in good health. The way she walked every day. She watched what she ate. You wouldn't think someone like that would have a heart attack."

"So she wasn't sick?"

"I guess she was, but I didn't know anything about it."

"Huh." Neither did Simon or Dina, apparently.

"But it could have been the War, you know."

"What do you mean?"

She knitted her fingers together. "Sometimes I think that we forget what that must've done to people, to their bodies, to be afraid, and cold, and starved for years. To live without knowing if they'd be killed tomorrow or even that very same day. To watch people beaten and murdered, and cities burn. Think of how devastating that would be to your body and your soul, the kind of assault that would be. So when someone like that dies forty, fifty years later, how do you know it wasn't the Germans who killed them?"

This was not something I wanted to speculate on, and I resisted the quiet passion in her voice. Then I wondered if Valerie had stayed in contact with my mother, had visited her here, to keep the connection open between *us*. I was touched, but Val having seen my mother so much made me feel even guiltier about having neglected her. And it made me wonder, too, why didn't she leave the German money to Valerie, to someone who obviously cared about her?

"What's wrong?" Val asked, eyes narrowing. She had always seemed able to follow my mood changes, the track of my thoughts, and it was both reassuring and a little creepy to find how little that had changed.

I told her about the Will, though I didn't mention any sums. Told her how perplexed I was by my mother's bequest to me.

Did Valerie have any guess why? "You talked about the reparations, about the War with her?"

"No, not much. Hardly ever, really. But she did think the name was terrible. "*Wiedergutmachung.*" Valerie said it carefully, as if each syllable were a stone she was stepping on to cross a stream. "Your Mom always thought that was idiotic. How could you make something like that good again?" She pushed her hair back off her shoulders, arching her back a little. "She said there could be no forgiveness, no making things good. I didn't try arguing with her. How could I? My parents didn't apply for the money."

My mind was wandering. In the kitchen that was so much a part of our past, I oddly flashed on the ways Valerie had picked on herself years ago, complaining about her skinny hands, her droopy earlobes, her thin lower lip. It all seemed ridiculous to me then, and more so now. Valerie had always carried herself well, and even slouching a little in her chair, she glowed, she had presence.

Dina always admired that in Valerie. Even though Dina was the more attractive woman, with what people today would call a Gwyneth Paltrow look, she had maintained that Valerie was something more impressive, more lasting. "Val's striking. Men give her a second look, Paul. She's deep—like a painting. And she always wears just the right thing. It gets on my nerves."

Another song Val and I had listened to in college was starting to run through my head: Iggy Pop's plaintive, drugged-out *Fall in Love With Me.*

"But maybe it was your Dad," Valerie was saying, and I snapped back to attention. "Maybe watching him deteriorate and then having to put him in the nursing home—that could have worn her down. She did seem depressed."

"How could you tell? Mom was always angry, or depressed, or both."

Valerie read my next question before I could get the words

out. "I visited your Dad in the home on his birthday and Father's Day, holidays, whenever I could. Your mother used to insist he knew when she was there, but I think she was just a little—"

"Crazed?" I suggested.

"No. A little too hopeful."

"Any kind of hope was crazy. His brain was fried. He was never going to get better. I saw him today. It made *me* crazed. It was a nightmare."

She said, "I know," but seemed far less upset. Perhaps because it hadn't been years since she'd seen what he had become. Maybe more frequent visits dulled the shock. It was not a theory I wanted to test.

So. Valerie, my ex-girlfriend, the woman I broke up with over fifteen years ago, even *she* had been more devoted to my parents, more dutiful, more respectful than I was.

I finished my drink, but I felt a bit wobbly when I tried to stand, and I didn't attempt making another. I must have been drunker than I thought, because I asked her if she remembered the night we'd seen Seiji Ozawa.

"You mean the night you almost proposed to me?"

There it was, then. "You knew."

"Oh, yes. You didn't have to say anything—I could feel it. You were like a high diver who keeps climbing the ladder, walking to the edge of the board, getting himself set and ready, then he turns back. Even looking straight at the stage I could feel you staring at me, sizing me up, then backing off."

The image fit. I could see myself stripped down to my Speedo, and Valerie as a gleaming pool of clear water, waiting.

"I wonder if I should have married you."

"That's your problem, Paul," she said with asperity, "You're still wondering."

Now I made it to my feet and came around the table, sat on the edge and took her free hand which she let me hold, while eying me warily. Her hand was as cool as her expression, but I didn't let either faze me.

"Val, remember the first time we made love here? In my bedroom?"

She shook her head.

"And we only had half an hour, and we kept the door open and put your clothes in the john so you could run in there if Mom came back early from her dentist appointment on the East Side?"

"Well, I was faster on my feet back then." She didn't smile at the reminiscence.

I asked her what was wrong.

"Your eyes. They're so desperate."

That was enough for me. I mistook her empathy for an invitation and leaned down to kiss her, but she pushed me back, gently. She rose and announced (still gently) that she was going home and would ask the doorman to hail her a cab.

I trailed after her while she retrieved her coat. No more happy puppy with lolling tongue. My tail and nose were drooping, my ears brushed the floor. "Are you busy? I'm not going right back to Michigan. Maybe we can have dinner."

"Possibly."

"When? Where?" I asked, sounding even to myself like an oaf.

"We'll talk," she said, eyebrows up, expertly unlocking the door and pulling it open. She slipped out into the hall to wait for the elevator. Considerately, she kept the door from slamming. The smoothness of her exit reminded me of all the times when we were dating and I'd waited down on Riverside Drive with her for the No. 5 bus to wheeze up and take her home to Washington Heights.

Weaving back into the kitchen to clean up, I suddenly felt foolish and even more solitary. I couldn't talk about this to Simon, it was embarrassing enough to have shared what happened with

Camilla. I cursed not having anyone in the city to call, any old friends I could get in touch with. I wasn't like Dina, who still talked to friends from third grade, kept track of moves, babies, promotions. I had almost always let connections fade without making an effort.

Then I let out a throaty whoop. Val was back! And it was amazing she wanted to talk to me at all after so long a time, and didn't seem to think I was just a worthless piece of shit. But wasn't I? Suddenly I felt like hurling the glasses against the wall and kicking at the table or a chair until something broke. I was an idiot—a fool. I made a pass at her and she hadn't even been there half an hour—how could I have misjudged her and the moment so completely? I remembered my father sometimes dissing people in Yiddish: *Azah balvan.* What a moron.

No, that wasn't even it. Val had pegged it. I was something far worse. I was desperate. She didn't have to say everything else that went with it. I was a desperate, lonely failure, with a job I did well but that meant nothing to me, facing middle age.

But she'd come to see me from Mrs. Gordon's, I thought defensively, pleading to an inner jury. I turned off the light in the kitchen and stepped back into the foyer which was still redolent of her perfume. I breathed it in as if I were a whacked-out adolescent hungry for my inhalant. It was an amazing scent: earthy and clinging, smelling almost as if it had been roasted somehow.

When the phone rang, my first ecstatic thought was "Val!" I rushed to the foyer desk, plucked the receiver from its cradle, almost sending the phone clattering over the side.

It was Dina. "What are you doing there?" she asked suspiciously. No hello, no greeting of any kind, just the query that implied I was prying up floor boards looking for hidden treasure.

I sunk into the desk chair, deflated. "That's why you called me?" She had probably tried Simon's number first, and he'd told her where I was.

Change of tone: now she tried to be sisterly. "I'm *worried* about you. I think it's morbid to be staying at Mom's."

"Morbid? Why?"

Dina sighed like a nurse with a cranky patient. "You avoid seeing Mom for years, and now that she's dead you move in? Isn't it kind of sudden?"

"Her heart attack was sudden. And I have *not* moved in!" I felt cornered, no more articulate than a frustrated teen vainly trying to explain himself to some authority, unable to light the words that would rocket up and dazzle everyone with their Technicolor clarity and truth. I was sputtering—I was a dud.

"If you're trying to establish some kind of claim. . . ." Dina warned.

"What are you talking about? Claim to what? The apartment belongs to Simon and he doesn't think there's anything wrong with my staying here."

She dismissed that: "Simon's a *schmatteh*."

I fought back my exhaustion and rallied. "Dina, why are you badgering me? Is Serge telling you to do this?"

Her angry "No!" made her sound like she'd just stuck her finger in a socket, so I assumed I'd guessed something. But she didn't back off. "You know, Paul, I can have the Will contested—"

"Under what grounds? You're nuts!"

"A good lawyer can find something. Do you really want to drag this out?"

I didn't, so I hung up, then took the phone off its hook so she couldn't call back and keep berating me. But as soon as I had, I regretted it. I was flushed, breathing hard, ready to explode. If I were back in Ann Arbor, I would have gone running to burn this off. I felt cheated, felt that Dina had won by making me angry enough to hang up, stealing my words.

She'd always been able to argue rings round me; why hadn't she become a lawyer where she could hypnotize and bludgeon people on a daily basis and get paid for it, be admired?

The German Money

I snatched up the phone and dialed Simon's number. The wary way he answered informed me he'd been waiting for the aftershock of Dina's call to me. I gave Simon a nasty précis of our exchange, which he listened to without interruption.

"That's just Dina," he said when I stopped like a suitcase snapping shut. "She loves to get upset. It makes her feel alive."

This was so on-target I chewed it over for a bit. But I wanted more than insights and assessments, I wanted to demolish her. "What the hell is her problem? Why does she need any more money? She has plenty of money!"

"That's exactly why," he said sourly. "She wants more." He was being unusually critical of Dina, and I ate it up.

"She always did," I said, remembering how as I child she had complained if one of us looked like we had a bigger portion of cake, or a larger pudding, or any treat. Simon had to be stopped from giving her some of his, and me, I would feel my fingers itching to do a Jimmy Cagney and shove my dessert in her face. "You want more? Here!"

"Don't pay attention to Dina when she gets like this," Simon was saying. "She means well."

"I don't think she does."

Simon ignored that. I guess he'd bashed Dina enough for one evening, for him. "I wish Mom had never applied for the German money."

I found it hard not to agree with him. But even though our brief conversation left me mollified and able to feel unwound enough to go to bed, I couldn't fall asleep. Though real estate was expensive up on Old Mission Peninsula because it was so close to Traverse City and Lake Michigan, with my inheritance, even after taxes, I'd have enough for a small house. It wasn't just a dream come true, it was deeper. I had been so in love with Old Mission I hadn't dared let myself fantasize having a place up there because I knew I'd never earn enough money. It had seemed cruel to toy with the idea.

But how could I use the German money for a house, for something so prosaic, or use it at all? How could I spend any of it until I understood why my mother left it to me? Thinking about Dina's threats, I was beginning to wonder if Mom might not have wanted to punish me for staying away, knowing it would cause trouble, burden and torment me, and divide us from one another.

God, could she have been that angry at me, that perverse?

And even if I did buy a house on Old Mission, or better yet, build one, what would be the point if I was always going to be alone? There I was, back to Val again. What did she mean by saying "Possibly" when I suggested dinner? "Ask her, Stupid," a voice piped up inside.

I didn't, but I got up to flick on the light and opened the closet door. I pushed aside all the junk until I found a small cardboard box at the back whose sides were about ready to give way. Sitting cross-legged on the blue-carpeted floor at the foot of my bed, I delved through what was left of my time with Val. I had burned all her cards and letters, and what survived of those years here was ticket stubs from concerts, and Playbills, some from shows we'd seen together, some from before I met her. I picked at the programs with a sense of stifled wonder, as if I were an archeologist unveiling signs of an unknown civilization.

It all brought back a cascade of scenes and the sense of being inextricably, almost sexually bound with Valerie when we went to the theater or opera. Alvin Ailey. Les Grand Ballets Canadiens' production of *Tommy*. A matinee of *Lucia di Lammermoor* at the Met, with the warm and passionate Beverly Sills, and splurging on dinner at The Ginger Man afterwards. *The Crucible. Deathtrap. On Golden Pond. Evita.* And the rock concerts: Elton John, Seals and Croft, Jim Croce, Black Oak Arkansas, David Bowie.

There were random postcards, too, from museums. We loved

the quiet Frick on Fifth Avenue, where we could lose ourselves in timeless study of the medieval enamels, or the mysterious de la Tour, or Ingres's Comtesse d'Haussonville with her sweetly cow-like face perched above yards of sky blue silk. Our favorite room had been the English-style library with its Romneys and Stuarts.

Underneath all of this stuff were *tchatchkehs*: a stiff necklace of white shell beads she'd bought me at Lord & Taylor and I'd never worn; a white alabaster elephant that was a souvenir from a trip she took with her parents to Mexico or St. Thomas or somewhere; green marble bookends shaped like columns. Was this all that was left of our five years together, and why was some of it so hard and unyielding?

I heaved everything back in the box and shoved it into the closet. I'm sure there were more relics in dresser drawers. Shirts or sweaters, unless I'd thrown them out or given them away. But there had to be books she'd bought me. I could pluck those from the low bookcase by the door and read the inscriptions if I really wanted to torment myself.

I shut off the light, crawled back into bed and tried jerking off, which used to help me sleep when I was younger as reliably as three milligrams of melatonin did now that I was older. But my cock was dead to the world before I was.

· · · · ·

Suitably enough, I woke in the morning from a bad dream, staring at the large LCD numerals on a dusty alarm clock. It was 8 A.M. and I was surprised I'd slept that long. Also surprised at my dream of being on a winter battlefield at night, barefoot, my legs and arms frozen, struggling to dig a trench in icy ground, but my shovel only striking sparks.

Lying in bed, stunned awake by the cold I'd only dreamt about, I worried at the image of myself shoveling. It felt artificial, melodramatic, almost as if it were borrowed from someone else's dream. Had I read an anecdote like that somewhere, or had I dreamed this image before?

The din of New York began to hit me, and drove me from bed to the shower, stopping to gaze at the hexagonal white tiles in the bathroom floor that had generations of dirt ground into them, and would never gleam no matter how conscientiously my mother, or one of the less capable cleaning women she could stand for a brief time only, scrubbed them. It was a very New York floor, I thought.

Brushing my teeth, I studied my face in the medicine cabinet mirror, stretched mouth and all, trying to decide whether I looked more like Mom or Dad, but stopped when I realized it was probably "morbid," in Dina's assessment. I snarled, recapturing my outrage of last night, but lathering up in the shower and dunking my head in the hot steady stream, my argument with Dina seemed childish. Maybe she did mean well. Maybe in her clumsy loud way she was trying to help. As soon as I soaped my crotch my cock leapt up as stiff as a highway police barrier. Thinking of Val in black, I pulled myself off with both hands as if I were wildly rowing myself to freedom. I came so hard I almost fell. It took a while to get my breath back.

Toweling my hair dry a little later, I felt even more charitable and putting up a pot of coffee to brew buoyed my good mood. When the bell rang, I reacted calmly, knowing that it was unlikely to be who I most wanted to say good morning to: Valerie.

It was Mrs. Gordon, balancing a silver cake plate covered with plastic wrap in her free hand. I took the platter from her and stepped back against the open door to let her in. Today her crinkly track suit was mauve.

"Coffee cake," she said genially, as if the words meant Good Morning. "Much better than Entenmann's—you'll see!" Wielding her cane as if she were a dapper old Edwardian gent, she headed for the kitchen. "Smells strong," she said approvingly. "I like strong coffee. How people can drink that instant dreck I don't know. Yech."

And as she settled into a chair and beamed up at me I thought that with her deeply companionable wrinkled round face—whose outlines were faintly blurred by tiny hairs you only noticed when the light hit them—it was actually Yoda in "Star Wars" that she resembled, cane and all, and not some turn-of-the-century boulevardier.

But if that made me Luke Skywalker, then what was the lesson I had to learn? Grinning, I carefully unwrapped her cake which looked so moist and luscious it could have been on the cover of a food magazine.

"Beautiful, huh?" she asked eagerly, and I agreed. "But wait till you taste!"

Serving us each a hefty slice, and pouring the coffee, I wondered what I would have been like if my mother had been as warm and relaxed as Mrs. Gordon. But then how many coffee cakes and rugelach would it have taken to fill me up?

I was probably romanticizing Mrs. Gordon, but so what? This ease of hers wasn't an act, and I felt her very real concern for me when I had another piece of the cinnamon-y, sugary, nut-rich cake, and unburdened myself about the German money, how it made me feel, how opposed I'd been to the very idea of it years ago, and now I was unexpectedly, deeply enmeshed in it.

"Yes," she said, daintily applying a napkin to her lips so as not to smear her lipstick, "I can see this is a problem for you." But she didn't sound entirely convinced.

"And you're sure my mother never mentioned it?"

"She was a very private woman."

"I can't understand why she left it to me."

"You're not Sherlock Holmes. Who needs to understand? Money is money."

"But isn't it—I don't know—tainted?"

115

"*Herr zech ein*, listen to me, even if the money feels bad to you, even if it *is* bad, you should take it."

"You think so. Why? Just because she left it to me?"

"That's a plenty good reason. But that's not all. You should take the money because something good should come out of evil. And won't your wife and children appreciate it?"

Shame-facedly, I told her that I was single.

Mrs. Gordon sweetly said, "I know that! But isn't it time you *did* have a wife and children? At your age, what are you waiting for?"

Well, I'd gone this far, I didn't see a reason to stop, and I had no one else to talk to, so I shared—in general terms—my rekindled feelings for Valerie.

"Here, I don't see a problem either. Love is love." She smacked her hands together to punctuate her point and I thought of Thelma Ritter talking about love in *Rear Window*, spurring Jimmy Stewart on to stop procrastinating his life away. Val and I had seen that movie at some revival house on Broadway, and afterwards I had thought of her as just as lustrous as Grace Kelly.

"You," Mrs. Gordon said forcefully, "you should forget about your mother's past. It's time you make for yourself a future." She nodded sagely, but with a faint smile as if to show me she enjoyed the phrase-making as much as giving advice.

But something gnawed at me. "Did my mother have any heart trouble?" I asked.

She frowned. "Of course! She had a heart attack. They didn't tell you?"

"But I mean before that."

She gave a very Jewish shrug. "*Ich veys*? Do I know?"

"She walked every day, in the park."

"I know. She loved her walking. But believe me, people die all the time when they look good and you don't expect it. My friend, the one who left me her apartment downstairs? I moved in with her as a roommate after her husband died. He was younger than your mother, and one afternoon he was going into the kitchen to get some milk. A glass milk, nothing fancy, and she heard him fall. Boom! Goodbye, Charlie! Happens all the time. You're here, then you're gone like nobody's business. Believe me, it's the best way to go. Fast."

I didn't ask for details; her brisk familiarity with sudden death upset me.

"Your father was an accountant, right? You're the same, huh? Looking at the details."

"Well, maybe." An accountant of books, I thought.

"Such a shame what's happened to your father." She sighed. "Terrible, terrible. To be alive, but not living. Your poor mother— what she suffered for him. But now that's over. It could be worse." She beckoned me over, quipping, "I need a lift." On her way out to get ready for what she explained was her daily little shopping trip, she wagged a shriveled finger at me and said, "Don't make yourself crazy over this business with the money."

After she left, I washed up while looking out the kitchen window to the mammoth brown and beige apartment building opposite, every window framed with different curtains or shades, it seemed, and each one opening up to different lives, floor after floor of them. It was a little less repellent than before. Was that Val's influence? Mrs. Gordon's? Or just all the sugar and caffeine?

I enjoyed being fussed over like this, baked for. It was fun making Mrs. Gordon smile, and giving her the chance to offer me advice which somehow didn't feel intrusive or rude. Of course my comfort with Mrs. Gordon was due in part to not having any history with her. She could have been an interesting stranger turning to me on a plane to chat and pass the time. Our interactions had the same sense of unexpected intensity and inconsequential charm. Or was it more than that?

I had bought myself time back at work. I was alone in my

mother's apartment. I was waiting for a call from Valerie though I had no idea when it would come. But I could always call her, couldn't I?

In my mother's phone book, where the entries were inexplicably made in hard-to-read pencil, I found a number for Val Hoffman and an East Side address. I memorized both of them, staring down at the small frayed page as if it were a medieval Book of Hours and I were the fond aristocrat who'd commissioned it. I ran a finger across her info and found myself wanting to lean down and kiss the words and numbers.

But I drew back at the thought that Mom had written this. Kissing anything of hers, anything that belonged to her, seemed not just outrageous, but undignified. That word. How many times had I heard her dismiss something as "undignified"? Her face would screw up and she always pounded on the second syllable, making you feel you'd been slapped. Strange that Serge's family had used the same label for Dina's job.

I drew back from the desk, thinking that Dina might be right, that I was suffering a fit of morbidity. Suddenly the apartment felt stifling and I thought of flying home that very day, but I wasn't ready. And even though Mrs. Gordon and Simon made sense about the need for me to move on with my life, wasn't that my problem? Hadn't I spent so many years trying to move on from Val that I'd actually stood still?

Simon had told me there was a gym near his place in Queens, and I'd brought my goggles, Speedo, key lock and my swimmer's shampoo. Now I dug out the Yellow pages to see if I could find a gym with a pool in my mother's neighborhood. It took a few minutes, and one phone call for a day's guest membership, and I was soon headed a half mile down West End. I had forgotten how hilly the street was, undulating up and down in a way that made the cars and cabs seem like part of a fun ride.

Something had definitely changed in me. Instead of feeling hemmed in by all the brick and limestone and granite that lined the street, offended by the pathetic treelets in their cruddy squares of earth, and bludgeoned by the noise, I felt strong, alive. It was the kind of solid rush I got after a good run on the high school gravel track near my apartment complex in Ann Arbor, or after seeing a movie that didn't demean the audience by offering blithe unrealities like breadcrumbs scattered to a jostling squad of ducks.

Improbably—to me, anyway—the gym was housed in the basement of a huge pre-Depression era apartment building whose elaborate facade teemed with carved faces and arabesques. The gym itself was pretty ratty compared to what I was used to, with battered freestanding metal lockers, weary-looking linoleum flooring and indifferently painted walls. Back in Ann Arbor, my gym was a combination of health temple and mini-mall: a brassy, flashy renovation of a two-story commercial building, where disco music wafted through the air like incense and members offered up their sweat to the Gods of Exercise. The West Sider had a hangdog feel, with even the few potted plants looking weary.

But my own gym was always crowded, no matter what time I went in, as if members were trying to fight the image of Ann Arbor as an intellectual haven. Crowding was so bad that sniping often broke out between people over use of a machine or even a set of dumbbells. The moldy West Sider was blissfully empty, and there wasn't anyone in the lap pool. When I slipped on my goggles, checked their fit and slid into the cool water, it quickly embraced me in the kind of swim I rarely had. Everything clicked for me that morning. My breast stroke was as smooth and confident as my butterfly and even my weakest stroke, the backstroke, felt solid. I swam slowly, not caring how long I was there, just enjoying the sense of connection with the water, enjoying even the smell of the chlorine. Often, when I swam, I felt like I was imposing my body, was somehow out of synch with the water. But not today. Today I cut through and kicked and turned as if the pool were my home.

When I pulled myself up out of the pool after what I discovered from the wall clock was an hour, I nodded at the wannabe Baywatch dude drowsily working as life guard, and headed off for my second morning shower, goggles down around my neck. The showers were as empty as the seedy locker room.

In the small steam room, I thought about our long ago summers in Far Rockaway, and Dad patiently teaching all of us to swim. You'd never have thought such a loud man could be so quiet, so steady, so willing to repeat himself without annoyance. It was the same when he taught us to drive, and looking back, I wondered which was natural, which forced: the heartiness or the muted concentration? I could almost feel his big hands holding me in place in the water while I had practiced kicking and stroking, and the first time he'd released his hold and I'd amazed myself by shooting off through the water until sheer joy and excitement made me bob up and laugh, "You let me go! You let me go!" I remembered his toothy grin. Those days at the beach had been infinitely more thrilling than learning how to ride a bike, perhaps because we were physically closer and it was as if his energy had poured into me.

Funny how I'd been swimming for years without thinking of Dad's role in it. I'd somehow managed to block that connection. I had never thanked him for his lessons, for his steadiness, for the gift. Too late. Like so much else in my life, it was too late.

And I regretted never having gone swimming with Val. I'd kept it jealously to myself, for no reasons I could clearly discern now. Quietly obdurate, I hadn't wanted to be on my high school's swim team, either, though I was fast back then and could have competed. What was I trying to protect? Privacy? Independence?

I walked back to Mom's apartment, or Simon's, a little drained by the swim, and sobered by the finality of death and disease. I'd always been so healthy as a child and as an adult, even before starting on flu shots in Michigan, where people tended to develop all kinds of allergies and sinus conditions popularly termed "The Michigan Nose." I'd never had an operation, never broken a bone. I had kept myself fit, and at forty-two was possibly in better shape than ten years before. My waist size was still 30 inches. Around me at the library I had been watching colleagues, and on campus and in town, acquaintances at the University, start to disintegrate. The women turning pear-shaped, their gait uneven and uncomfortable-looking, and their faces grew lines of wear or bitterness at the betrayal of time; the men's bodies blossomed with paunches that threatened their belts and always won, their faces reddened and pouchy or white and wasted. For so long, I had felt quietly superior to these signs of decay. But who was I kidding? I could end up like Dad, and it could come on earlier for me than it had in him.

Unless I went like my mother. Boom. Goodbye, Charlie.

Riding the elevator up to my mother's floor, I decided to call Val and leave her a message. I went straight to the phone and dialed the number without having to consult my mother's address book.

But a machine didn't take my call, Val did: "Paul? Is that you?"

I gulped.

"Paul?"

I started to ask how she knew it was me, then figured it out: "You've got Caller ID."

"Good detective work."

I hesitated. Wanting to phone Val, I'd imagined listening to her message and leaving a brief one of my own. But now we had to have a conversation, and it was one thing to see her last night, another to deal with only her voice. I felt both surprised and cut off. Then I heard myself say, "I was just thinking about my Dad," unable to pick something trivial out of the air. I relaxed, and my shoulders came down from up around my neck. It felt good to have said that to her.

"It's awful, isn't it? Looking at him and remembering how lively he was."

It wasn't the word I would have used, and Valerie seemed to sense my disagreement. "That laugh of his—"

"He laughed a lot," I agreed, sourly.

"He was no picnic," Valerie offered.

"Oh, he was. A picnic with ants, food poisoning and a thunderstorm."

Valerie ignored my bitterness. "He went through a lot," she said. "In his life."

Letting go for the moment, I nodded as easily as if we were sitting on a park bench enjoying a lazy Sunday. Fifteen years since we'd really spent time together and it was feeling anything but stiff; the silence that opened up between us now wasn't at all tense.

"So what's it feel like being at your Mom's?" she asked.

"Strange," I said. "Lonely. I feel like I have to stay here, to— I don't know, to discover something."

"About her, or about yourself?"

"Hell, if I knew that, I think I'd already be ready to go."

"Maybe you're mourning, since you missed the funeral."

And Val hadn't, I realized just then. Simon hadn't mentioned her presence, and whether he was hiding it from me, or just protecting me, I felt patronized. Didn't he think I could have handled the information? Or was it just another example of honesty disappearing into our family's emotional Bermuda Triangle?

"You're home," I said to Valerie, back to my surprise that she'd picked up the phone.

"Where did you think I worked? I'm a writer."

"I never thought about it." To recover from that gaffe, I tried a joke: "The jury will disregard the last remark."

Valerie didn't laugh or make a quip of her own. Very seriously, she said, "Paul, I'm not judging you."

"That's good." I thought I should quit before I said anything else stupid, so I asked her about dinner that night.

"Well. . . ."

I suggested one of our favorite places way downtown. "Is it still open?"

"Oh, yes, and still reasonable."

"So?"

She sighed. "Let me think. If I get—I can meet you there at 8:30."

"Great! I'll let you go, now," I said. But when I hung up, the phrase seemed an unfortunate one. I didn't want to let her go. I didn't want to repeat the mistake I'd made once before and regretted more deeply now than ever. But what did that mean, exactly, and did I really have any say in what happened now between me and Valerie?

It seemed wise that she had arranged for us to arrive separately. It gave me, at least, more time to settle into this very new reality. I had always drifted back to thinking about Val between relationships, but had never gone far enough into fantasies to have imagined conversations with her. Though when Camilla had recently tried to register us for a Nouvelle Swing class at the gym, I'd resisted because I'd remembered how much fun it was back in the late 70s and early 80s doing the Bump and the Hustle with Val. We weren't very good, but we laughed a lot. I hadn't ever minded dancing with other women, but it wasn't something I'd seek out, and I'd also suspected Camilla would approach the class with the single-mindedness she had for sex, turning it into a part-time job.

Back in my room, I picked out a few old disco albums to play, starting with Carol Douglas's *Midnight Love Affair*. Val had mocked its plangent busy strings and the inane lyrics, even though she loved dancing to it.

With the record thumping away, I headed for the front of the apartment as if the music had somehow given me permission to intrude. My mother's small bedroom smelled both musty and sweet, and the shade was drawn. I left it down, and stood inside the room surveying the ornately-carved old mahogany bedroom set that had belonged to Dad's cousins. The pieces were too big for the space they dwarfed, leaving hardly any place to stand. On the shelf built into the headboard were Mom's prize mysteries, books by Agatha Christie, Ngaio Marsh and Dorothy L. Sayers. I surveyed the lurid and silly titles: *False Scent, Elephants Can Remember, Strong Poison, Appointment With Death*. My mother was always rereading these hardcover books, which puzzled me, since none of them seemed substantial enough to me to stand the real scrutiny you'd give a book on your second time through. And what was the point anyway, once you knew who the murderer was? Mom also had well-worn paperbacks with less familiar titles: *Unorthodox Practices, Likely to Die, Shadow Image,* and I knew that she visited a mystery book store on Broadway, Dina once having told me that our mother liked mysteries set on the Upper West Side. I couldn't imagine it was an especially crowded field.

I opened up Dad's closet next, and as if a body had fallen out, I jerked back, startled. There was nothing there. The tie rack inside the door was empty. Likewise all the cedar shoe racks, and the hangers. No jackets, no suits, no pants. Just a patina of dust. Mom must have thrown his clothes out, or given them away. It shocked me, because he was still alive, at least his body was. And it made me sad. She hadn't waited for him to truly die, for Simon and me to paw over his clothes and perhaps take something for ourselves, something we might not wear but would keep as a souvenir, hanging in a closet as a reminder or a totem.

But I didn't blame her. I could see my mother, enraged by fate, ripping all his natty, well-cared for clothes from their spots and tossing everything onto the bed in a sacrificial pile. It could have been like my burning Val's letters, an attempt to break free that was doomed. For me, the act of destruction wasn't more than the frenzied barking of a dog on a brutally short chain trying to reach a tormentor. I had achieved very little destroying Val's writing to me, and now regretted what I'd done.

Dad's side of the chifferobe was empty, too, which made Mom's seem weirdly overstuffed. I carefully lifted every item, every scarf, every lace-edged slip, every girdle, possessed, I realized, by images drawn from movies. When people died there was always something profoundly dramatic that popped up in an ordinary spot. But I found nothing in her drawers or her closet when I shifted through each dress, each bag, even inside the shoes hanging on the door in bags, and the hat boxes on the higher shelves. My hands were starting to smell like the lavender sachets scattered through her things.

What would happen to all this stuff? More to the point, what would happen to all *my* stuff if I walked into the kitchen like Mrs. Gordon's friend's husband and dropped dead? I'd never even thought of making a Will.

When the phone by the bed rang, I jerked back and stared at it for a few rings before I answered. It was Simon, saying he'd dropped off a fare not too far away, and did I want to have lunch with him. He offered to pick it up, and I said that was fine. I put Gloria Gaynor on when Carol Douglas was done, and hummed along with *Never Can Say Goodbye*.

He showed up less than half an hour later, looking a bit like Dad, I thought, in a tweed blazer, maroon and gold tie, and a blue buttoned-down shirt.

"What's that music?" he asked, bemused. We had a lot to talk about, but I let him proudly unwrap the pitas, cream sodas, and the big black and white cookies (one for each of us).

"Remember these?" he asked eagerly. I did.

We set out place mats on the dining room table. He sat at one end and I sat to his left.

"I'm glad you're staying here," he said, mouth full.

"Why?"

"Because I think Mom would like it."

I didn't know about that, but I did realize that when people died, there was nothing to stop you from attributing thoughts and feelings to them—who could say you were wrong?

I thought he probably meant that he liked it that I was in her apartment, but the next thing he said changed my mind.

"She knows you're here."

"Don't be weird."

"I can feel it." He chewed solemnly.

"What else can you feel?" I asked, trying to keep my voice from expressing any doubt or criticism, even as I dreaded what he might say next.

"That she's still here."

It was all I could do not to laugh or look under the table. I decided not to pursue the topic any more; after all, I wasn't running a talk show.

"Dad's clothes are gone," I said.

"I know. After Mom and I picked things out for the nursing home, she told me she gave it all away to Goodwill." His eyes were tight. He shrugged. "That was Mom."

Now it struck me less as an attempt at self-preservation, keeping herself from being pulled under by the disaster of his illness, and more like something ruthless out of a Greek tragedy. Medea killing her own children.

"He doesn't need all that stuff any more," Simon reasoned. "Mom was his wife, so it's her decision. I mean, it was. . . ."

The mood lightened as we bit into our black and white cookies at the same time and both said "Yum." Mouths full, we grinned at each other like little boys. I was eating more in New York than I did at home. I was far hungrier.

"Do you like living in Michigan?" he asked, with the curiosity of every native New Yorker who thinks that living elsewhere isn't much better than setting up house in a ditch.

"I do. I'll spare you the civic booster speech, but the people are friendly, and it's a beautiful state."

"But isn't the Klan there? And Militia groups? I read about them and it scares me."

I was touched. And perhaps in response to that, a cynical voice said inside of me: "So scared you couldn't pick up the phone?" God, that was my Dad talking. Time to change subjects and kick him out: "I saw Valerie last night."

Simon swallowed hard. "You called her?" He sounded almost hopeful.

"No. You did. And she decided to come over."

He nodded, perhaps waiting for me to turn on him.

I laid out all the rest of it, dispassionately. "Val went to the funeral. Val used to visit Mom here all the time. She goes to see Dad at the nursing home. Nobody told me. It's like she's been part of your lives all this time I've lived in Michigan." I didn't know if I was angry or envious, but even as I tried to decide, I was aware of how much my life had changed. I was talking about Val, about my feelings, with Simon, who had always seemed so closed off and inaccessible, a turtle, surly and remote.

"Kind of," he admitted. "But it was mostly Mom. I hardly ever see Val or— I still like her, though," he added, as if I might accuse him of disloyalty to one of us.

"So do I."

His eyes lit up. "Really?"

"She looks great, doesn't she?"

He nodded. "Her hair's long again. She had it really short and it didn't suit her. Made her look too serious."

"What do you know about hair?"

He snorted. "More than you, bro. Gay men *invented* hair."

Now I laughed at Simon's foray into camp. "But you're only half gay if you're bisexual."

"God, you sound like Dina. She always has to have the last word."

Chastened, I said "Sorry" and then told him I was having dinner with Val at our old hangout.

"Wow."

"Yeah, wow."

"What's going to—? Do you think—? Will you—?"

"I want to talk to her more about Mom, that's the first thing, since she saw Mom every few weeks."

"Valerie said that?" He shook his head. "I didn't know it was that often. More than me or Dina. Way more."

"Did you read Val's memoir?"

He nodded. "It was pretty good. I've read books about children of survivors, you know, how their parents can be over-protective and stuff like that. How it's hard for the kids to pull away."

That didn't seem entirely true for the three of us. Dina became a romantic Jesse James; I went to Michigan; Simon joined what was left of the Sexual Revolution.

"Am I in it? In Val's book?"

"No—it's all about her and her Mom and Dad, and it ends before she met you."

"Has Dina read it too?"

"Sure."

Dina and Simon and thousands of other people, strangers, knew more about Valerie than I did, had shared more of her life than I had. But it was my own fault.

I must have looked distraught, because Simon reached over and squeezed my arm.

"Whatever happens," he said. "At least you loved her, and she loved you."

It was surely meant as comfort, but it sounded like an epitaph, and there was something valedictory in the way he clasped my hand.

I pulled him out of his chair for a hug. We stood, arms around each other. I asked him if he remembered when we saw *Death of a Salesman* and how upset he'd been afterwards.

"And I crawled into your bed, like when we were kids and used to tell each other riddles," he said quietly.

"I felt really awkward," I said.

"I know. The way you looked at me in the morning, like I did something gross. But I understood. You've never been very physical. Just like Mom."

"Like Mom," I echoed.

"Can I sit down now?" he asked, and I let him go. Then, since we were raking up the past, I explained that I'd also wondered about that night after the play, and if he'd been—

"Attracted to you?" He looked amazed. "Are you nuts? You're my brother!"

"Good. Keep it that way."

"Besides," he blurted, "I don't like men who are big. For some things, small is easier to manage. What can I tell you?" He leered: "It's my nature."

I laughed at the tag line, but his revelation was more than I needed to know, and probably more than he wanted to share, because he blushed, and as if signaled, we started bussing the table. Still, his remark had set me musing. Looking at another man, Simon would probably want him to be what he wasn't, someone to complete him or balance him. In that sense it was the same as being attracted to a woman. Was I a quick study, or what? My father had a sarcastic Yiddish phrase for just such an obvious moment: "*A choocham a Yeed!*" Roughly translated: You're some smart Jew.

Simon said that clearing the table had reminded him of the first time he and Janet had friends over to dinner, how nervous they'd been, and how everything had been fine until it was time to clear the table. "And Janet just looked at me and said, 'I'm a person—I don't have to do that.'"

"Another therapy victim," I observed, but I was just tossing off a cliché. That whole part of his life seemed unreal to me.

"I guess."

"So what happened?"

"Well, we got divorced." He smiled. "But not for that."

"It seems such a long time ago," I said.

"Not long enough."

In the kitchen I told Simon that it seemed like I'd been spending most of my time back in New York eating and doing dishes afterwards.

"What's wrong with that? I'll wash up and then I have to get back to work."

While he was in the bathroom, I thought about him, about us. I could imagine other occasions like this—sharing meals, talking, searching each other out. I couldn't call it coming home because I don't think I'd ever been "at home" with Simon. Maybe I should invite him to visit me in Michigan. We'd spent more time together in the last few days, talked more and said more to each other than we had in the last decade. I could either lament having taken so long to get here, or savor it and try to build something.

Visions took me over of showing my brother the state I had fallen in love with and never wanted to leave. We could rent a tent and drive around the state in my new Grand Prix with the sunroof open and the Bose stereo blasting. The sights unreeled for me like a travelogue: Sleeping Bear Dunes, the Grand Hotel, the stunning long Mackinac Bridge to the Upper Peninsula, Tequamenon Falls, the hills of Houghton-Hancock, the view from beautiful and desolate Copper Harbor in the Keeweneau. Michigan had three thousand miles of shore line and we could see as much of it as we wanted. It felt almost like passing something on to another generation.

My first year in Michigan I had been quick to notice people react defensively when I said where I was from, as if I were some Ruritanian Inspector General out to demolish and suppress a pretentious bunch of provincials. And the New Yorkers I met in Ann Arbor did tend to act like life had betrayed them

by sending them into exile, however briefly. But I was so eager
to adopt a new home, so eager to escape, that it came naturally
to me to gripe about the traffic and the noise, the rudeness of
New York. Complaining, but about New York, not Michigan, I
was halfway to acceptance. I got all the way there by describing
without exaggeration my first sunset over Lake Michigan. I was
camping south of Charlevoix and the sky that day seemed to
have been sliced open, laying bare layers of violet, sienna, and
crimson like rocks in a deep canyon. I carried that vision with
me the way people have a lucky charm or a mantra.

"This was great," Simon told me, collecting his stuff from the
foyer desk.

"Definitely." We might have been laying some kind of curse
by affirming how good the time together had been. But before
he left, I had to ask him something that had just occurred to me.
It was gruesome, but I needed to know the answer. "Your messages just said Mom was dead. Did she die alone—in her sleep?
Was someone with her? Were you the one who found her?" I'd
been uneasy about raising any of this before, but surely that
couldn't be taboo now.

"Uh-uh. It was Mrs. Gordon, checking on her because they
were supposed to be going for a walk. Mom didn't answer the
phone, so Mrs. Gordon came upstairs and found her. She was
the one who called 911."

"Mrs. Gordon got the super to let her in?"

"I don't think so. She probably had an extra set of keys for
emergencies. Some of the older neighbors died or moved away,
so I guess Mom must have picked her. Gotta go, kiddo." He'd
never called me that before; I liked it.

We hugged again, this time more formally, like diplomats
making a point for their respective nations, but I was a little
uneasy, and unsure why. When the door closed, it didn't take
long to sink in. My mother had asked me to return my keys
when it was clear I'd moved to Michigan permanently. Yet here

was someone she'd only known a short time who was intimate enough with her to have access to her apartment, something I wasn't allowed. Another punishing little reminder of the costs of keeping my distance.

I may have been sleeping here, eating here, trying to learn something by going through her things, but I was just a transient. Just like my mother. She had a husband, children, a home, what most people would call a life, yet wasn't there an insubstantiality about my mother herself, for all the heaviness in her voice, the rooted way she could stand in a doorway and stare her censure? The War, the unspoken, had made her something of an automaton, an inauthentic human being. So why bother trying to pin her down?

Yet I couldn't draw back from whatever search I was on.

I grabbed the keys, and out in the hallway locked the door several times to make sure I was doing it right. When the elevator came, I asked Tommy what apartment Mrs. Gordon was in, and he frowned when I thanked him and headed for the stairs down to 3E.

She was in, and after some slow unlocking of what sounded like five or six locks, she pulled open the door and beamed up at me. "Boy, am I surprised! Come in, come in." Her enthusiasm contrasted so sharply with my mother's typical cold reception on seeing me that I felt a wave of regret as hot as nausea sweep through me. I instantly covered my face, but there was no need since I was behind Mrs. Gordon, who was wielding her cane a bit unsteadily, leading me from a dark narrow foyer into a small cramped living room. Dickens, I thought. Fringes and velvet, flocked wallpaper and doilies, patterned lamp shades and dried wreaths, gleaming round tables with clusters of porcelain shepherds and milk maids, heavy curtains and drooping house plants.

"None of this is mine," Mrs. Gordon said, perching on a throne-like chair, her feet on an ornate tufted footstool. "I sold everything in my house in New Jersey, or gave it away. It was time."

I sat on a stiff, camel-backed maroon settee, thinking that a woman any larger than Mrs. Gordon might have succumbed to claustrophobia here. I certainly felt hemmed in.

"Not like your mother's apartment, hah?" She grinned, eyes crinkling. "No view of the river, first thing. And then all these *smochtehs* and *trantehs*." She shook her small head ironically. "So *ungemacht*."

I looked to her for a translation and she summed it up: "Overdone, crap. But it was Dora's, and her children didn't want it. They didn't even want the apartment—can you believe such a thing? They told her to leave it to me. It's nice to be so rich you can give away an apartment. One boy, he's a cardiologist, retired already, lives in Palm Springs, he has Jaguar cars," she said. "The other one, he's on Wall Street, has three houses. Could be four. My memory's not so good for some things."

She clasped her hands on her lap and looked around her as happily as if she'd carved every curlicue, every tiny heraldic shield or gryphon. "It's ugly. But after a while you get used to it. Besides, I won't be around forever, so. . . ." She gave a good-natured shrug, and then said, "My God, you come to make a visit and I don't offer you tea or nothing."

I tried to keep her in her seat, but she grabbed up her cane and bee-lined for the kitchen from which she called out to me progress reports on the kettle, the plates, even the knives and forks. I could have been some furious potentate whose minister was trying to placate him by soothing inanities.

Glancing around the overstuffed, over-decorated and over-heated room, I found it emblematic of my time in New York, which was so much a place of interiors it made Ann Arbor seem like Big Sky Country. No wonder Woody Allen had called one of his movies *Interiors*.

"Mrs. Gordon, do you need help?"

"You don't get up yet! You're my guest!"

But I did get up. Across the room I saw a recent photograph of my mother, framed in silver. It was taken at what looked like a street fair. Behind her was a crowded frieze of children with balloons, handholding lovers, stalls selling t-shirts or ethnic foods. Mom at a street fair, not a scene I would have imagined before. She looked quietly distant, but at least neutral, wearing a dark fur coat and matching beret that made her seem foreign and a bit mysterious. But pictures of Mom always struck me as mildly mysterious because each one highlighted the absence of photos in her life. Dad had several creaking albums with opaque brown paper covering each page charting his extended family's move to America, along with some grim studio portraits taken in the Old Country. My mother had no album, no pictures. The Nazis had been very thorough.

In high school, Simon had once made me read passages from a history of the Holocaust by some French historian describing how the Nazis had not just slaughtered Jews, but pillaged them like some ancient barbarian horde. We'd been arguing about the Volkswagen Beetle, which I thought was cool, and Simon said he could never own anything made in Germany. I told him that was bigoted.

To shut me up, he thrust the paperback at me, and I read not just of gold fillings, money and gems, but suitcases, linens, glasses, furs, shoes, clocks, pens, wallets, pipes, silver, pianos.

"What if you went to Germany and you stayed in a hotel and in your room there was this old candelabra and it was Mom's— stolen from her house."

"But I'm not going to Germany."

"When you buy something they made, you're dancing on Jewish graves. They murdered six million Jews and stole everything of theirs that wasn't nailed down. Paul, they took combs. Combs! The whole country sits on a pile of Jewish loot."

I gave him back the book, unconvinced at the time, but his

passion and the images in that book worked on me slowly, and eventually I'd find myself surreptitiously checking the underside of a clock or whatever to see where it'd been made. I still did it, now and then, but had never told anyone. It wasn't a subject that Mom or Dad had ever raised, but I'm sure she felt the same way and kept it to herself.

Doing a family tree project in third grade, I'd been shocked to have her tear the colored paper from my hand and snap the ruler I was using in half. "There's nothing!" she shouted. "Nothing left. Nothing to talk about." Handing in the project with only Dad's family filled in, I'd been terrified and humiliated, expecting a bad grade, but it came back with a check mark and no comment from my teacher. Years later, Dad told me he'd called the school and explained that my mother couldn't talk about her family and why.

Mrs. Gordon was still fussing in the kitchen.

Mrs. Gordon had a set of keys. Mrs. Gordon had a picture of my mother that she had taken, or gotten a copy of if a street photographer had taken it. My mother had figured in Mrs. Gordon's life, while I had been trying to squeeze her out of mine. I had never hung up or put out a picture of my parents, as if I had no antecedents, as if I were an American pioneer of the last century fleeing a murky past for the tabula rasa of the West.

Mrs. Gordon called me into the kitchen. Following her sweetly punctilious directions, I brought in a steaming tea tray with *"ungemacht"* china cups, tea pot and sugar bowl, and a plate of Russian tea cakes.

"Green tea," she said. "Good for your health. Your mother she drank it all the time. She loved it."

That startled me because it was new, and it was significant. Desperate for a topic during a phone conversation some years ago when I'd called to wish her a happy birthday because I hadn't gotten a card off in time, I had preached about the benefits of green tea and echinacea with goldenseal. My mother had scoffed: *"Green* tea?" But she had apparently taken it up. I felt mildly dizzy, realizing I'd had an impact on her in something, wondering if she thought of me when she drank it. Not that the tea had helped her any.

Mrs. Gordon poured some of the fragrant tea for me and I took a tea cake on my plate, then added two more when her incredulous glance admonished me. "What? You're worried about getting fat? Nooooo. . . . Not in a million years. Don't be stingy with yourself," she warned me, waving at the little cookies. "You're away from home, you should have some fun, especially since—"

She let the sentence hang.

"My mother used to make these sometimes."

"I know."

What else did she know about my mother? I bit into one of the almond-flavored tea cakes, trying not to get the powdered sugar all over my chin. Mrs. Gordon watched me with the quiet, slightly wide-eyed delight of a grandparent, and I basked in it. I had never known grandparents, never had entertaining allies who could defend me to my parents, that is, when they weren't telling me how lucky and spoiled I was because life was so much harder for them when *they* were young. It was a clichéd vision, but one I had craved no less for that.

"So," she said cheerfully, "You have questions?"

"How did you know?"

"Your eyes."

First Valerie, now Mrs. Gordon commenting about what they saw in my eyes. It made me want to put on sunglasses.

I started slowly. "Simon told me you found my mother. Was she—"

"Already dead? Yes."

That meant no last words, no deathbed lament or invocation, no message that would in effect come from the grave. We had stopped talking years ago, so why was I hoping for even a scrap, when it might not have been what I wanted to hear? And if she'd said something wonderful or inspiring or forgiving, wouldn't I feel guilty and stung? It seemed pathetic either way.

"I'm so glad Valerie was here, it would have been awful by myself."

"Val was here—there? Where was she?"

"She came by my place to try to convince me to talk to her about the War. For her new book. Interviews, or something. When they were taking your Mom away is when she showed up. Terrible. *A gantzeh iberdreyenish.* What a mess, with the ambulance. . . ."

Val hadn't mentioned this, neither had Simon. I put it aside, forging ahead with more questions even though I felt squeamish asking them. "Where was she?"

"Your mother? Lying down on the couch. Maybe she was taking a rest before we were going out. She used to get tired."

That didn't exactly jibe with Mom's vigorous daily walk, unless that was a front and she hadn't wanted anyone to know she was actually fading.

"You checked her pulse?"

"Of course," Mrs. Gordon said gently, humoring me. "But it wasn't necessary."

"Why not?"

"Where I was in the War, I saw plenty of death. Believe me, you don't forget what it looks like. A stinking barracks or a comfortable West Side Avenue bed, death is the same."

"I thought you said she was on her couch?"

She shrugged. "I'm old, I mix up words all the time. You'll see, it will happen by you, too."

"I wish I'd been there. At the end." I sipped my tea. "You didn't tell me yesterday you found her." It came out almost harshly, but I didn't apologize.

Mrs. Gordon seemed unperturbed. "Of course not. I didn't want you should be upset. It's not something pretty."

Well, that stopped me as solidly as driving into a snow bank. She was right, but even though I didn't want to know any more grisly details, I resented being treated like a child by someone I had just met. Why did people hide things from me?

"You feel guilty," Mrs. Gordon observed. "You miss her."

I nodded dumbly.

"So do what she wanted," Mrs. Gordon said, clanking her cup down in her saucer like a Munchkin judge with a pint-size gavel. "She left you money? Take it, go back to Michigan. Live. She wanted you to live."

"My mother told you that?"

Mrs. Gordon shrugged. "*A voo den?* What else? It's not obvious enough? She knew what you needed. She wanted to make you happy. You don't leave somebody a lot of money for no good reason."

Of course, that was the obvious explanation. But my mother treating me generously in her Will, wanting to make my life easier? Improbable. Then I asked Mrs. Gordon how she knew it was a large sum.

She threw up her hands. "Doesn't take an Einstein. You would get so upset if it was *bubkes*? Beans?"

I granted her that. "You've met Dina, right?"

She nodded. "Oh, sure," she said, with a neutral tone I took to be critical, given how cheerful she usually was.

"Dina wants me to give the money away, or split it among the three of us." I don't know if I was asking for advice or just talking to myself with an audience.

"It's nice to want things."

"But—"

"What's the problem? You think she's talking sense?"

"No. I think she's angry. And jealous."

"She's already rich. Giving her more money won't make a difference. This girl, her problem isn't money."

That was certainly true.

"You know, Paul, the old commercial for the airline, it goes 'Some people just know how to fly?'"

"Northwest," I said, not adding that in Michigan we called the airline that had a lock on Detroit flights "Northworst" because of its crummy service, late arrivals and poor customer relations. Northwest had turned the entire state of Michigan into fodder for a talk show on business abuse.

"Some people know how to live," she said. "And some don't. Some complain no matter what happens to them. Look at your mother. Did she complain? Nooooo. . . . My husband died of liver cancer, the chemotherapy made him sick as a dog. He never complained. Even when he was dying, he knew how to live."

"But it's more than complaining or not complaining, isn't it?"

She shrugged and waited for me to elaborate, but I wasn't certain I could. I'd harbored a similar belief about knowing how to live ever since I'd broken up with Val and left New York. In the years that followed, when I let myself explore the inner battlefield I had both created and fled, I came to believe that there was something missing in me. In me, and in Dina and Simon. That all three of us were hamstrung in slightly different ways. Unable to take hold of life, or at least our best opportunities. Simon was sullenly self-destructive, Dina was a theatrical and questing malcontent, and I was a saboteur, methodically destroying my own happiness.

Look at where I was now. My mother had left me enough money to live out my stifled dream of having a home in one of the most beautiful parts of Michigan, yet I felt totally unable to celebrate, to accept the gift and enjoy it. Instead, I felt burdened, crushed, conflicted. Wouldn't other people be wild with joy about this good news?

Mrs. Gordon seemed to be on the edge of falling asleep. I drank some more tea, wondering what it would take for me to embrace this reversal of fortune.

Mrs. Gordon shook herself a little and said with a self-deprecating smile, "I was just resting my eyes."

"You need the rest—all that baking."

"Noooo. . . . I love it. And it gives me pleasure to see you enjoy yourself."

"Do you have any children?"

Her face closed. "I couldn't. The War made it impossible. Nick was everything for me. But after he died, I decided I was gonna live. I wasn't ready to give up yet." And she reached into her track suit pants pocket, brought out a wad of pale blue tissues, pealed several off and blew her nose.

"I'm sorry I brought it up."

"How could you know?"

This seemed a good time to leave and with equally specific instructions, I brought our tea things back to the overcrowded dark kitchen, Mrs. Gordon following me with her clumping cane.

I bounded up the stairs to Mom's floor, remembering how much fun it had been as a child to race Simon and Dina on these same stairs, flinging ourselves around the corners at each landing while Mom commanded us to slow down or we'd kill ourselves. The clatter of our shoes, the gasping and shouting. I remembered the times I'd half-reluctantly, half-excitedly shepherded Dina and Simon down to the park on their tricycles, enjoying the responsibility and control, but resenting being bound to them when I would rather have been upstairs reading a library book on dolphins or World War I or UFOs.

The message light was on and there was a brief request from Dina for me to call her at her Quebec City number. I'd only seen pictures of that home once: a lovely three-story early 19th century white townhouse with cerulean blue shutters and flowers spilling from the flower boxes, set like a diamond in a severe-looking narrow street whose homes had much less interesting and playful facades.

The German Money

Dina had first met Serge in Quebec City, vacationing by herself, practicing her French. She made it sound like a scene right out of a movie, Audrey Hepburn, perhaps, in *Charade* being hit on by Cary Grant. Dina, in a black velvet mini dress and black leather boots, had been sipping a glass of Bollinger on the terrace of the amazing Chateau Frontenac Hotel, watching the jugglers, singers, acrobats, and other street entertainers on the mammoth boardwalk below, when silk-suited Serge had appeared at her table and said in English that he'd like to buy her a bottle of whatever she was drinking.

"He looked good enough to eat," Dina had recounted. "No, better than that. You'd want to save some for later. But I was pissed off he tried me in English. I was feeling very chic."

Cooly, Dina had responded in what I imagined was a Sharon Stone voice, "*Monsieur, vous pouvez parlez en français, car je le comprends, et ç'est la langue du pays, hein?*" Her accent and her request for him to speak in French because she knew what was Quebec's language won her even more points than her looks. They were soon done with a bottle and having dinner at one of the city's most famous restaurants, À La Table de Serge Bruyère. It was an eleven-course meal, or so Dina said.

"Elegant, sure. But like boot camp!" Dina laughed when she'd told me. "The maitre d' and waiters patrolled the rooms like sentries, and everyone whispered. Amazing food, though. And people flew in from Paris to eat there all the time. The French Foreign Minister was across the room—he waved at Serge! I was impressed."

The word made me, oddly, think of press gangs in the British navy kidnapping people on the high seas.

My mother had all our numbers set up for speed dial on the living room phone, and I called Dina back in Quebec City.

"How are you?" she asked, and I was pleased her first thought wasn't Simon, though I wondered how sincere she was. I brought the phone over to the window seat and sat down.

"I'm okay. I was downstairs talking to Mrs. Gordon about Mom."

"Do you like her? She's kind of nosey."

"I've only met her a couple of times. But, yes, I like her. I think she's very warm, and Simon keeps saying she was kind to him at the funeral."

Dina paused as if about to contradict me, but then settled for dismissing Mrs. Gordon with "I guess she's okay."

"She was Mom's friend," I pointed out.

"She seems to think so."

"What's *that* mean?"

"I don't know, I don't understand old people. But I never got the feeling they were bosom buddies or anything. Mom didn't mention her much at all."

"Mom wasn't big on talking about anything," I said.

"Well, that's true."

I remembered Simon telling me about survivors when he was immersed in Holocaust reading in high school, how they often kept their past to themselves, how the trauma made it hard for them to open up about the war or anything. It explained my mother, but why couldn't she have been different, an exception?

"Mrs. Gordon found Mom." I said it as if I had to hear it again to believe the reality of my mother's death even though I'd been to her grave.

"Right. Simon told me a little. It's not something I wanted to hear."

"She let herself in when Mom was late and didn't answer the phone."

Dina snorted. "Mom gave her a set of keys? Mom never gave any of the neighbors keys—she didn't trust them. She always said she hated even the super having keys, like he'd spy on her or something."

Though Dina had seen our mother more often over the last

fifteen years than I had, even she hadn't visited as often as Simon had, and thus neither of us could make statements about her, her friends, or her habits with any real authority. Mom had gotten older, Dad was in the nursing home, she could have decided she needed to feel safe, prepared for an emergency. I ran that by Dina, who seemed reluctant to admit that she had not been in constant contact with Mom.

"But it doesn't matter," Dina said. "Mom's dead and it doesn't matter who found her or how. Why are you hassling that little old lady? What's the point? Why don't you just go back to Michigan?"

"I'm not ready. And why are you pushing—is there something you don't want me to know? I mean, nobody told me Val was practically living over here, or that Mom had heart trouble. What else has been going on?"

"Mom didn't have heart trouble, she had a heart attack. You're being paranoid." Dina breathed in sharply and I could tell she was going to really blast me. "Tell me what the hell are you trying to prove down there? That you're a good son?" she jeered. "Excuse me—isn't it too late for that?"

I matched her sarcasm: "And you were a good daughter?"

"At least I didn't stay away for years at a time."

"Well, whatever you did, Mom didn't think it was so great since she left Simon and me both more money than she left you."

Dina hung up, and with the echo of the slammed phone in my ear, I felt anything but proud of myself. This was no victory. We'd been squabbling like kids in a sandbox smacking each other with their shovels and pails. What could be more disgustingly childish than claiming "Mom liked me best!" And even worse, I'd said it without believing it. If we'd been on the phone any longer I probably would have bragged about going to see Valerie that night and how much nicer she was than Serge. Ridiculous. Our mother's death had not brought any dignity to my relationship with Dina; instead, it had sent us rocketing back to childhood pettiness and rage.

But there was more going on. Sitting there staring at the phone, I realized for the first time that Dina and I had been re-creating the way our parents had sometimes interacted, only in a cruder form. Mom would calmly drop poisonous inflammatory statements that eventually made Dad explode. I remember once when they were going out to a party and she looked Dad over and asked if he was going to wear that blazer.

"Of course! That's why it's on my back!"

"If you want to look like that, go ahead."

"Look like what?" he snapped.

"A peasant."

He was in and out of three more blazers before they left, his face brick red.

We had been watching this personal Pay Per View show for years—was it any wonder it had infiltrated our lives? Dina's language was fouler and my fuse longer than Dad's, but the pattern was there, and even Simon played the same role with us as with them when he was around: neutral, distraught observer.

I checked my watch. Only a few hours before I'd be having dinner with Val. Would she be able to help me unhook from any of this and understand my mother's Will? I'd loved Valerie's common sense years ago because it was never brutal, but she wasn't the Wizard of Oz, just Valerie, and maybe she wasn't even interested in my problems. Maybe she was just being kind. I knew who she had been; the woman she had become was still a mystery.

Dina's insults galvanized me to go to my mother's phone book and check for her doctor's number. I hoped it was still Dr. Stein, who had seen all of us for years. He was a bearish, gloomy-eyed, barrel-chested man with a heavy, arm-waving, bent-back gait and rumpled suits, given to clichés, but we all liked his gruff-ness, and one touch of his heavy, hairy hands always convinced me I was going to get better, no matter how sick I was. Their weight carried tremendous conviction.

When I dialed his number I did get a nurse, so that meant he was still practicing, but her voice was unfamiliar. I expected to be told to try him another time or even to be blown off altogether, but my timing was—for once—perfect. I'd caught him between patients, one of whom was late, and I got right through when the nurse told him who was calling.

"Paul?" came Dr. Stein's incredulous rumble. "Long time, no see. Sorry about your mother."

"Did she have heart trouble?" I asked without making nice first or even asking how he was.

"No. She was in fairly good health. She boasted about it."

"But she had a heart attack."

"Paul, your mother wasn't a spring chicken. She was getting old, and let's face it, her life wasn't any bowl of cherries."

Was that a reference to the War, us kids, or Dad?

"She made a big mistake trying to take care of your Dad at home, but even if she hadn't done it, hey, dementia can crush your spirit. Like watching someone disappear in quicksand. I've seen it destroy the one spouse who's well."

"But weren't you surprised? I mean, she exercised every day."

"She took walks, Paul. That's all. And the famous runner, what was his name, Jim Fixx, back in the 70s? Was he in good shape? Of course he was. The best, fit as a fiddle, but he dropped dead anyway. He was running! We all die, son. Ashes to ashes and dust to dust. I'm surprised your mother held out as long as she did. She was a very troubled woman, very unhappy."

"Was she taking anti-depressants?"

"Wouldn't touch 'em, but I kept telling her to try. You can lead a horse to water," he said, not bothering to finish it. "What's bugging you, Paul?" he asked belligerently. "Why all the questions? When was the last time you saw her, anyway?"

Apparently everyone in New York knew what a lousy son I'd been. Humiliated, I squeezed out thanks for his time, and only after I hung up did I wonder about asking to see Mom's medical records.

That was crazy. It would make him think I was questioning his judgment and he might even suspect I was sniffing around for a malpractice suit. I was trying to get closer to my mother through all these questions, to make up for the years of emotional and physical distance, but it wasn't really possible. Somehow, fifteen years had rushed past without my ever admitting the possibility that my mother could die before we had a chance to restore some real connection between us. We'd exchanged birthday cards and calls, and I sent flowers on Mother's Day, but what little warmth might have been there long ago had dissipated.

I could still remember her contemptuous question, "Michigan? You're going to do a degree there? In library science? How can libraries be scientific? It's nonsense!"

Forget that the University of Michigan had the country's best program. My mother was devastated, taking it personally that I'd dropped out of Columbia's English Ph.D. program, sick of all the theorizing that made people unnaturally value critics over writers. The turning point hadn't involved a professor or a class but another student, a whippet-thin preppy with Long Island lockjaw who'd seen me reading *Middlemarch* and had said, "You read *primary*? How retro!" I knew then it was time to get out of Columbia.

Dad had been slightly more good-natured about my decision, until I added that I was breaking up with Valerie. That's when he joined the anvil chorus, both of them pounding away at me. "Michigan? Who goes to Michigan?" And then he used the Yiddish word for crazy people: "*Michigoyim*, that's who! Hah-hah-hah!"

I had felt stifled in New York, hoping that flight would bring me release. What a crock. In college I'd made my slow way through Henry James's *The Ambassadors* in a senior honors seminar. The protagonist's cry to a young man to "Live, live all you can," had struck me as embarrassing and creepy back then, almost like the ravings of some homeless man yelling at you on a subway platform. But now it resonated painfully. I wasn't nearly as old as Strether in that novel, but I hadn't lived much either, and I'd missed too many chances.

Musing over this, I'd been leafing through the address book, and found a listing for a Bruce Menzies, Attorney. I didn't know for sure if that was Mom's lawyer, the one who'd written her Will, but I gave the number a try. A flat-voiced secretary welcomed me to a multi-named firm and put me through to Menzies' voice mail when she said he was unavailable.

I left my name and my query: had he handled my mother's Will, and if so, could he answer a few questions for me. When I hung up, though, I wasn't sure what questions I would ask him if he called back.

Overwhelmed by the day's uncertainties, I decided the only smart thing to do was to take a nap. I set two alarm clocks, one in Dina's room, one by my bed, to make sure I was up in time to meet Val for dinner. After fifteen years, being late would have been horrendous.

But I needn't have bothered setting the alarms because the phone woke me an hour or so later. I staggered from the bedroom down to the kitchen in time to hear Valerie's voice leaving a message: ". . . so if you want to stop here first, we can go downtown together." I snatched the receiver from the wall phone.

"Val—I'm here. I was asleep."

"Oh, good. You looked pretty tired last night."

Last night, I thought, puzzled. It had been less than twenty-four hours since I'd seen Val. . . .

"So did you hear what I was saying? You did? Good. I got

more work done today than I expected and I was able to ar-range— Arrange things, and I could use the break." She gave me her address and when I hung up, I was stunned. We were getting together earlier than planned. She was inviting me over. We weren't meeting on neutral ground or, more accurately, in the past. She was letting me see where she lived *now*.

I showered again just to wake myself up, and changed clothes, wishing I'd brought something snazzier than the black jeans and blue cotton cableknit sweater. But when I showed up at Val's door a half hour later, she nodded her approval; she had always liked me in blue.

Joe Jackson's romantic jazzy *Night and Day* was playing on the stereo—I took that as a good sign; gangsta rap or Marilyn Manson would have been discouraging.

In Val's gleaming-floored large living room, there was a huge display above the fireplace on a brick wall: at its center hung the cover of her memoir, framed, in a nimbus of what I guessed were reviews and feature articles from various newspapers and magazines. I didn't step closer, to keep from seeming nosy, but I could make out that the dust jacket featured a sepia-toned photo of her as a little girl with her parents, all of them smiling somewhat tentatively. It was very appealing, and a little sad, perhaps a photo taken their last day at a favorite vacation spot. It wasn't one she had ever shown me.

I was once again ashamed not to have heard about her book. If it had been me publishing a book, I'd be very offended about her having missed something so big in my life, even though we had been living very separate lives. It seemed obvious that her book and its reception were as dramatic and life-changing for her as if she had been married and had a baby.

I turned from the wall and she wasn't looking at me, but eye-ing her plaudits with quiet satisfaction. "There's more. I just framed the best."

"I feel really bad that I didn't—I didn't know."

She nodded.

I couldn't help thinking that the living room and dinette filled with Mission-style furniture and decorated in rust and gold were a perfect backdrop for her coloring. If I said that, or told her it was all beautiful, would she think I was sucking up to her?

Across from the fireplace, the wall was solid shelves and many hundreds of books jostled each other there for space like Japanese commuters on a train.

"Review copies—the best thing about reviewing. People send you books all the time. It's like living in a fairy tale. You know: Once upon a time there was a little girl who longed for her own library. . . ."

"Do you still review much now that your book did so well? Do you like reviewing?"

"I do it a lot, and I love it. Tons of free books—and people pay you to express your opinion—and then you get your name in print. What could be bad? Now, how about a drink? You must like Scotch, living in Michigan. I have Laphroig, The Macallan, Dalwhinnie. . . ." There was something disinterested in her tone, as if she were holding herself back, or entertaining me at someone else's behest. She was in a good mood, but it didn't seem to have much to do with me.

I opted for Laphroig and settled onto the couch, watching Valerie in the Pullman kitchen. She wore a body-hugging glittery black sweater, black clogs and a forest green suede skirt and looked sexy and proficient, completely at ease with herself. It was a sense of comfort I wish I was experiencing myself. When she turned, her hair swung from side to side just like a goddamned shampoo commercial, though not exactly in slow motion, of course. I could almost feel the soft weight of that mane when it had tumbled onto my face, years ago, and onto my thighs. She came over, handed me my drink and sat facing me on one of the chairs.

"You know, Michigan isn't that cold," I said. "You must be thinking of Minnesota."

She shook her head. "I never think of Minnesota."

"Not even when you saw 'Fargo'?"

"Especially then." She looked down her nose at me and grinned.

I drank half of my Scotch.

"Hey, slow down," she warned, crossing her legs.

"I'm trying." I felt as excited as if we were on a first date: flushed, expectant, worried. But maybe it was more like a last date, Val's chance to finish what had been left up in the air when I decamped from New York. Which would actually mean it wasn't really a date at all, just a lousy postscript. I had not called her from Michigan after I left, or written any letters; I'd wanted a clean break as if such a thing were possible.

"Isn't it funny," she said, sounding like someone at a boring party deliberately looking for a conversational topic. "About Scotch? And cigars? They were so uncool when we were in college. I mean, Nixon and Kissinger, that's the kind of people you'd imagine enjoying a shot and a stogy. The Trappings of Power," she intoned like a CNN anchor trying to make the trivial momentous. "Now they're back and they're hip."

I pointed to her clogs. "So are those."

Val waggled her uppermost foot. "Everything comes back, doesn't it?"

"Like paisley ties. That's been twice, now, or more."

"And psychoanalysis—it's really big again."

"Have you—?"

"No. But I did go into therapy after you left. After we broke up, actually. Before you left." She smiled as if mocking her own journalistic exactness. Then she shrugged. "You would have, too, if you'd stayed. At least eventually."

"What do you mean?"

"It's a law now. Everyone has to do therapy in New York.

That's why there's so much less crime."

"I thought it was more cops on the street."

"No, it's more insight."

This was good, this was very good. I'd tensed up when she mentioned my leaving New York, but now we were joking together. Keep it going, I thought.

"Even Sinatra's back, but I guess it helps that he's dead," I observed.

"Well, I don't think people are going to be drinking sloe gin fizzes the way we used to."

"God, those were disgusting." I pictured us laughing at some bar with big round Irish Coffee-size glasses set in front of us, holding those pink sweet drinks. On the CD player, Joe Jackson was singing about being in a taxi with his love. "What a great album," I said.

"Classic," she agreed, and we both listened to the music for a while, letting its driving beat fill the room and the evening. That would be us in a little while: stepping out, into the night, just like Jackson was singing.

"You're wearing Angel again," I noted.

"I don't wear anything else."

"It's terrific."

"Men love it, that's what the guy at Bloomie's told me."

"A guy sold it to you?"

"I guess he was a diversity hire at the perfume counter," she threw off. "I wanted something new, and it had just come in."

Men liked it. Which men? Had she bought it for someone particular? That was not a question I could justifiably ask, so I asked her "What do *you* like about it?" to keep the focus on her and on me.

She looked off to the right, considering, then turned her eyes back to me. "I like it because it lasts."

I'm sure she didn't intend that as a slam, but I felt guilty, again, for having abandoned her. I suppose it was natural for

the simplest remark of hers to trigger regret and embarrassment, but I hated the way it stung. I almost felt that the question of our future seemed to lie there on the table as if it'd been
dropped like our check by a careful waiter making sure it was
right between us. Who would be the first one to reach for it?

Neither one of us, as it turned out, because the momentum
was taken over by the CD's shift to the next track.

I wanted everything to be perfect, and I wanted life to match
the song Jackson had been crooning, so I asked her what her
view was like. After all, she was on the tenth floor.

Val disabused me. "It's not worth opening the blinds—just
some more apartment towers like this one, mostly." Hers was
covered in that hideous glazed white brick that had always
struck me as more appropriate for a Roman vomitorium than
a high rise, but a lot of developers on the East Side had clearly
disagreed. "How are you doing with Simon and Dina—that's
got to be hard."

"I've had some good talks with Simon."

Val looked surprised, no doubt remembering my old sense of
frustration with his inaccessibility, and his general stoned air.
"And Dina? Still feisty?"

"Feisty doesn't touch it. Try arrogant. Having a rich husband
brings out the worst in her. And speaking of rich people, I'm
surprised you live over here."

"Why. Because it's sterile and snobbish?" she asked.

"That's a good start." Growing up, I'd always subscribed
to the distinction that the West Side was warm, human, and
cultural, basically everything the East Side was not, despite
the presence of the Guggenheim, the Whitney, the Frick and
the Metropolitan. And Val, living in Washington Heights, had
seemed to agree, at least that's what I remembered. Strange to
have grown up mocking New Jersey on one flank and the East
Side on the other. Even stranger was having moved to Michigan
and fallen in love with the beaches, the state parks, the expansive

sand dunes, the Great Lakes, and that breathtaking drive across the eerily long Mackinac Bridge. New York had been the center of my universe and I'd grown up with the firm belief that you couldn't survive anywhere else, yet Michigan had knocked that chip off my shoulder.

"Oh, I don't buy into the crap about the East Side any more," Val said. "This is a neighborhood like any other neighborhood." She slung back her drink. "Come on, let's go get some dinner."

Had I offended her? Val scooped up a black leather jacket and I felt hustled out of the apartment. But maybe I was over-interpreting things.

In the cab speeding down to the Village, I tried not to react like a wimp as we jolted and lurched in and out of traffic with head-hammering speed, but it was a hell of a ride. You could have thought we were in a movie, being pursued by someone who had cried "Follow that car!" Had I ridden cabs years ago and never noticed the streets were so rough and the ride so dizzying? Maybe back then, as a student in college and then graduate school, cabs had seemed exotic compared to the subways or buses, and I'd simply screened it all out.

Thinking of bad roads, I remembered one night on a wildly jostling bus ride cross town through Central Park on the way to a party, well into our second year together. Val had suddenly looked alarmed and I squeezed her hand to reassure her we'd be okay. "I'm not scared," she had whispered. "I'm—" and she glanced wildly down at her legs crossed in super tight jeans and then up at me as if playing a frantic tiny game of charades. As her face reddened with embarrassment, I realized that the pressure at her crotch was just right and all the bouncing up and down was going to make her come unless we stopped soon. The bus heaved to its stop sooner than we expected, and Val and I kept cracking up all night when our eyes met at a party. The quiet anarchy of our joke saved us because the hostess was having some kind of argument with her boyfriend and kept insisting on playing the Stones' *Under My Thumb* on the record player. "Good song," Val had said later, "bad vibes." "Well at least nobody got stabbed," I had pointed out.

Sitting a foot or two away from Valerie in the cab, enveloped by her presence and musing on our past, I wanted her. Not the way I'd wanted Camilla and other women, to prove my mastery, to *make* them come, but to hold her, to feel connected, retrieved, and forgiven.

"Tell me what you do at the library. You're in Special Collections, right?"

From the sublime to the ridiculous. I wrenched my thoughts back to work, while lights blared at me from every store window we passed.

"I do different things. I spend a lot of time on the computer handling inter-library loan requests. And we keep vertical files on various topics and I sort clippings, pamphlets, leaflets, filing the material by subject. I also help order books for the rest of the library, so that involves reading *Library Journal* and other trade journals. And sometimes I do trouble-shooting—looking for materials that've been misfiled by student assistants."

"Sounds a little, well, dry."

"Most of the time it is. Desk shift is what I really enjoy, because then I'm working with people, some faculty but mostly students."

"Let me guess—they're doing papers and they want your help?"

"You got it. The first thing they need is help figuring out what they want because they have such broad topics."

"So it's like teaching."

"Right, except the job market's always been better for my field, and you don't have to duke it out with Marxists, structuralists, feminists, queer theorists, post-modernists."

"But I bet you would have been good with students."

In college, journalism had been Valerie's goal, and teaching mine, which is why we'd both gone on to do graduate work at Columbia. But I was unhappy there, and had given up that dream entirely, never really sure how much of a loss it was. I would never teach, but in the years since Columbia, I'd watched academia get bashed by the right wing and undermined by skirmishing over political correctness, with bean counters taking over administration, trying to turn students into customers and faculty into intellectual sweat shop workers. It wasn't an edifying spectacle.

"I deal with some faculty and alumni, some people from the community, but mostly students. That's really the best part of my job—helping them figure out what they need, what they should be looking for and writing about. And lots of students have no idea how to work with books—or whatever—you can't remove from the reading room. That can be a hassle because it turns me into study hall monitor. I have to point out that they can't bring in pop or pizza into the reading room, they can't put their elbows on rare books, they can't rip out pages or write on anything they're consulting."

She looked incredulous. "Do they try?"

"Absolutely. They think they're at home and it doesn't matter what they do. This one kid yelled at me when I saw him about to scribble in something, 'Why are you persecuting me? I wasn't going to write in *your* book!'"

"That's wild."

"Then there are the sullen middle schoolers with their Moms riding herd on them, or guys who won't let their girlfriends talk for themselves. You know, the kind of guy who holds his hand at the back of his girlfriend's neck, and answers whenever you ask her a question."

Val shuddered. "I hate that. You never did that."

Score one for me.

"But is it fun? Is it enough?" she asked. "You don't sound

that satisfied." The observation was kind but a little stern, as if I'd let her down. What exactly had she been thinking my life was like all these years? If she saw my mother regularly, she must have known I was only a jumped-up librarian, but perhaps she'd assumed it was somehow more meaningful work.

I didn't know how to answer her questions. I'd spent over a decade of my life at a job that was in some ways only a higher version of working as a checkout clerk. It demanded very little of me, and gave me even less. But wasn't that how most people lived? Who said work was supposed to be fun or satisfying? Tolerable seemed a decent bottom line, and there was nothing about my current job that I couldn't tolerate. Still, saying that to Val would have been difficult, since she was successful, had been reviewed well in the *New York Times*, and that was the ultimate imprimatur in New York, the ultimate benison. She had stayed in New York and made it; I had left and made nothing but tracks.

And more dispiriting as we rode south through the gleam and roar of New York was my sense that the work I'd described to her wasn't just unexciting and even grubby, but in a way, insubstantial. I'd been wasting years on it.

"I always thought you might become a writer," Val said.

"Why?"

"The way you stood back and observed things."

"Even you?"

She laughed lightly. "Yes, even me."

"I liked writing about nature when I was a kid."

"Really? You never told me."

"My mother didn't think it was worthwhile—and I was only a kid, what did I know?"

Valerie shook her head. "Do you think about it now?"

"Sometimes."

"What would you want to write about?"

"That's easy!" I launched on a rapturous description of Old

Mission Peninsula, of the cabin I'd stayed at, the vineyards spreading over low, undulating hills. I told her about Chateau Chantal, the winery and bed-and-breakfast on 65 acres near the peninsula's northern end where the microclimate was actually similar to part of France's Bordeaux region. At the center of vine-covered hills, the turreted main building looked like a Swiss ski lodge, offered gorgeously comfortable suites, a mammoth fireplace out in the timbered great room, and stupendous views. I'd checked it out, but had never been there for more than a stop to taste their excellent Pinot Noir. I didn't come out and say so, but I figured she'd realize that I wished I had someone to share it with.

Valerie took it all in, smiling, nodding, enjoying my enthusiasm, but when she spoke at last, I was disappointed. I was hoping she'd say she would love to see the peninsula and Chateau Chantal some day. Instead, she just commented, "It must be beautiful."

I had been trying to win her over and counter the image of myself as having grown dull, as having no potential, but her remark deflated me, like babbling on to some English snob who greets your recitation with a flat "How interesting" before turning away. I could have just handed her a brochure and let her file it.

I fell silent, and observed the streets, the cars, the incredible variety of people out there. They were so bizarrely different from one another it made Ann Arbor feel very bland and homogenous, an academic theme park. Val seemed to have withdrawn. This was not good. Until my tourist bureau misstep, I had been quietly basking in something I hadn't felt in many years: a warmth and ease that pulsed slowly through my body like a drug. Years before, with Val, I had felt settled and happy, comfortable. Leaving New York, leaving her, I had never found that peace with any other woman. It was pretty simple, and desperately complex.

Perhaps sensing the mood change in the back seat, our Sikh cab driver switched radio stations from some droning talk show to something livelier, and Val laughed at the music that came up: Blondie's *Heart of Glass*, their first big dance hit.

"That song! Oh, my God," she said, laughing and wriggling her shoulders and head like a *Solid Gold* dancer.

"The first time we heard it we were in a jeans place on Broadway, remember? And the clerk was shaking her butt when we walked in."

"Yes! She was black, right? Medium Afro, thigh-high black boots. God, we were just kids," Valerie marveled. The three of us had boogy-oogy-oogied at the counter to the infectious beat and dopey lyrics and I remember the song buoying my whole day.

The cab pulled up to the Odeon restaurant on West Broadway and in much better spirits, Val and I split the fare. "Good luck," the cabby said when I handed him a generous tip. He seemed as knowing and benevolent as a crystal ball reader foretelling good news and fortunate events.

Once a cafeteria, The Odeon had been a restaurant for a while before we found it by accident one weekend back when we were dating. Though Val told me the long rectangular mirrors hanging high up were new, it looked and felt familiar to me. The glossy dark paneling made the large high-ceilinged room with a bar at one end feel intimate, as did the low-hanging fans and the four pillars that divided up the space. Val and I had always sat at a black and burgundy vinyl booth at the back with a view of the kitchen doors.

The sleek, black-suited maitre d'—who glided over to greet us so smoothly he could have been on wheels—greeted Val by name, then gave me a friendly once-over that I resented as much as his obvious long-standing acquaintance with Valerie. So she must come here a lot, I thought, and the suggestion wasn't really nostalgic for her. Looking around, I could count on one hand the people not wearing black; likewise the unpierced and those without dramatic hair. I felt like a hick.

But that passed when our coats were taken away and we were at our former favorite booth and checking out the view. "I once saw someone from *Law and Order* here," she noted. "One of the DAs. Do you watch that show?"

"Not really."

"I like the way the stories can start one place and twist into something completely unexpected. Oh—before I forget—" Val reached into a pocket and handed me some keys. "I meant to give them to you yesterday. They're your mom's."

"She gave you a set?" I must have sounded really envious, because Val just nodded and turned to perusing her menu. After we hashed over our choices, Val asked how I was doing, and I knew she wasn't just making conversation.

"I'm still trying to figure out her leaving me the German money. It's a lot of money, almost too much." I felt embarrassed to say exactly how much—it would have seemed like bragging. "Can you think of a reason why she did it?"

"Several." She peered at me over the top of her menu. "She couldn't leave it to your father, right, because he's so sick. You're the eldest. Maybe it didn't mean much before, but things change when people write their Wills. They can get very traditional, maybe even feel sentimental."

That was not a word I'd ever have thought of applying to my mother, but then I wasn't the one who'd been visiting her over the past fifteen years, and going shopping with her. At the end, Val probably knew Mom better than I did. Despite myself, I felt irritated at the thought. It was almost as if my mother had adopted a daughter. Wait—had she possibly felt guilty about that, and left me the money to make up for it? Boy, I was reaching there.

Our leggy waitress—in black, of course—brought water and described the evening's specials with shy grace that matched her Julia Roberts curls. Val suggested we have the gravlax and grilled tuna, and that was fine with me and our waitress. I suggested a bottle of Pinot Grigio and we were alone again.

"Okay, why not split the money?" I said. "Give it to the three of us, equally."

"That would never work. Your mom didn't trust Simon enough. It's not what she said about him exactly. But whenever he came up, it was almost as if she was wary."

"But he hasn't been doing anything wild for a long time. And he has a steady job." I was thinking of the car accidents, the divorce, the debts, his not finishing college, the drug dealing the police had luckily never nailed him on—that was what we knew about his past. There was doubtless more and worse that we didn't know.

"He's bi. Your mother couldn't deal with that. She thought he was unnatural. She never used that word exactly," Valerie rushed to explain, "but it was pretty clear. So I guess she felt she had to leave him something, but not the most. Not what she left you."

"And what about Dina?"

Val smiled indulgently. "Dina doesn't need as much. She's set for life."

"Mrs. Gordon said something like that."

Valerie leaned forward. "Your mom also could have left you the money because she loved you. Think about it."

"No way. She was so cold."

Val sighed. "You don't know what the War did to her. But even if she was like that before the camps, so what? Not everyone can be Mother Teresa or Princess Di. People do the best they can as parents."

I could not accept that. It was too forgiving.

"You think she loved me? Really?"

"Oh, yes. Much more than Dina or Simon. She may not have demonstrated it or talked about it—that wasn't her way."

I thought of Dad's jovial "It's my nature."

"Why are you so sure?"

"Because, of the three of you, you're the one who's most like your mom and she knew it."

This was not an observation that brought me any peace, especially since Dina had mocked me with the claim that I had become as distant as my mother was.

"Do you think I'm aloof?"

Valerie pursed her lips and replied with the dry humor of a physician whose patient can't seem to remember all the symptoms that brought him into the doctor's office in the first place. "Are you kidding? You've always been looking at things from a distance, holding back, you know that, just like your mother did. You've never been able to totally lighten up, to let go. When we were dating, it was—" She hesitated. "It was intriguing, I guess. Romantic, maybe. You keep asking why your Mom left you the money. Don't you get it? You're as critical and unhappy as she always was." She shrugged as if saying, "No offense."

Val was right, but it was even worse than what she said. I had somehow *chosen* unhappiness. I had fled her and reality and had settled in a college town, a place of transients and adolescents, where nobody knew me well, where my life was shallow and unreal. People bragged in Ann Arbor of having come there to go to the University of Michigan and stayed for the rest of their lives. It was a local mantra, being proud of having sunk into quicksand.

I couldn't face any of that, so I pressed her to explain why she didn't tell me she was there when my mother died, or soon afterwards, anyway. That she had seen my mother's body taken away on a stretcher, a scene familiar to me from countless news reports and television shows that had never seemed real before, but was now searingly intimate.

Eyes down and clearly uncomfortable, she said, "I didn't want to upset you."

Just like Mrs. Gordon, I thought. "I don't get it, Val. Am I a mental patient who could snap with one wrong word? Does everyone have to treat me like I'm going to fall apart if I know what's going on?"

"Paul," she said soothingly, "there's nothing going on. But even if something *was*, you're not the easiest person to tell things to." It was the kind of maddeningly quiet voice bound to push my buttons, probably anyone's buttons, and I was about to accuse her of infantilizing me, but the waitress brought our wine. We watched her deftly uncork it and pour; I said it was fine and Val and I drank without toasting.

"You didn't get married," I said out of the blue a few moments later over our appetizers, and Val's startled grin made her look like a criminal caught lying on the witness stand.

Then she relaxed. "That makes two of us."

"I never came close. You?"

"I did. It was well after you left. A journalism professor at Columbia." I must have looked cynical because she assured me that they started dating well after she was done with her degree. "I ran into him on the West Side, and he remembered me."

"What was he like?"

She pursed her lips. "Your basic cliché. Older, tweedy, balding. A Philip Roth type, but without the warmth." And when I must have looked blank, she said, "That was a joke. Roth isn't very warm. . . ."

"So what happened?"

"We were together, I guess you'd call it, for a couple years, and I found out he was sleeping with one of his students. Not very original, I told him." She sounded dispassionate, like a much older woman reviewing her *amours*, sorting through lovers as if arranging a vase of flowers. "Don't worry, this isn't going to turn into that scene in *Four Weddings and a Funeral* where Andi McDowell lists all her lovers and winds up in double digits."

"Does that mean you haven't had that many?"

"It means, even if I did, I'd keep it to myself." She pushed her hair back off her shoulders and with her arms up and breasts jostling, I imagined slipping my hands under them and burying my head in her cleavage or stroking her nipples with my thumbs, just brushing the tips. As if picking up my thoughts, or simply reading my eyes, Valerie crossed her arms over her chest.

I did a rough tally of my own girlfriends in Michigan. At grad school I'd plowed through a whole office of teaching assistants where I was the only guy, just to see if I could, but slowed down afterwards to one or two women a year.

"Adding them up?" she asked slyly.

I nodded.

"Well at least you didn't cheat on me. I'm grateful for that."

I didn't volunteer that I had never cheated on a woman. What was the point? What would I have been proving? Sure I loved looking at other women, but I waited, since I almost always knew in advance who I'd be putting the moves on. One of the raft of University of Michigan teaching assistants I'd slept with, Alice, had said to me when we broke up, "You scope them out in advance, like a croc hitting the weakest wildebeest of the herd crossing the river." I had laughed and snapped my teeth at her, but she wasn't kidding, and she wasn't amused.

"This guy, do you ever see him any more?" Maybe it was a lousy question, but her reference to my not having cheated left me unnerved. Though a compliment, it threw the rest of my behavior into unflattering high relief. That damning "at least."

"Steve got a job at Berkeley, so I don't see him, but—" She flushed.

"But?"

She breathed in as deeply as someone about to take a dare. "I see his face. Libby looks a lot like him."

"Libby."

"His daughter. My daughter." Though her eyes met mine defiantly, I felt anything but combative at that moment. Flattened was more like it.

"You have a kid." I folded my hands in my lap, then wondered why. I felt like everyone in the restaurant was staring at me, mocking me.

"She's seven and a half. She has a sleep-over with my folks tonight. They're back from Florida. She loves spending time with them."

"Why haven't you said anything about her before?"

Frowning, she looked out blankly at the other diners, and pulled her hair together with both hands as if wanting to twist it into a pony tail. She relaxed, let her hair loose, ran her fingers through it, and when she turned back to me, her face was soft again, open.

"How would you have felt if she was there when you came over tonight? Or if I'd brought her with me yesterday?"

It was my turn to look away. I couldn't imagine someone else in Valerie's life, someone always around. In my fantasies, she was waiting for me, untouched by time or circumstance, and we would pick up from fifteen years ago.

"*That's* why," she said, as if reading my mind.

"Do Dina and Simon know you have a daughter? Did Mom?"

She nodded. Of course they did.

"God, I feel like a chump. Why didn't anyone ever tell me?"

"What for?" she snapped. "What would it matter?"

I couldn't answer that because it was too big a question. "I didn't see any photos of her at your place."

"That's typical. You weren't looking. They were all over. I bet you missed the DVDs, too. *Lord of the Rings, Shrek, Monsters, Inc., Bambi.*"

Now I felt as if she'd smacked me. I remembered the large television, but not in any detail.

"I didn't bring her up before because I didn't think I had to."

"But she's part of your life."

Val nodded, letting me fill in the rest of that. I was not part of her life. She had a child, a career, and I didn't fit in at all.

I felt a little dizzy, and drained, as if I'd just swum to the point of nausea. I wiped my forehead with my napkin. "You hate me."

"Maybe you hate yourself, Paul."

I was torn between wanting to leave and wanting to put my head down on the table and sleep away this sudden nightmare. Valerie was a mother. Was I supposed to ask to see a school photo? Baby pictures? How was I supposed to behave now?

We were as blank for a while then as those long-married couples you see in restaurants who barely meet each other's eyes after they've ordered, and whose tables are toxic with silence.

"I talked to my mother's doctor," I said, when the appetizer plates were cleared and I had to say *something*.

"Oh. Did it help?"

"What?"

"Did it help? That's why you've been asking so many questions about her, isn't it? To feel at peace with her death, and your inheritance. You weren't here when she died, you never got a chance to repair your relationship with her, and you don't feel worthy of her gift to you."

It was a dismal catalogue, and I nodded, not adding that I hadn't even been a good enough son to return her phone call from a few weeks back.

"Sooner or later, you have to stop asking questions," Val pointed out, face open and reasonable and concerned.

"Even if I don't get answers?"

"Who said there were answers to this kind of stuff? But even if there were. . . . Have you seen *Arcadia*? It's the Tom Stoppard play, they did it here at Lincoln Center. Someone says that after we find all the meanings and explain all the mysteries, we'll be all alone, on an empty shore." She shifted focus, looking right at me now instead of at a scene of the play. "Do you want to be all alone?"

I shook my head, incapable of speech.

"Go home, Paul," she said gently. "Go back to Michigan."

"Don't you want me to stay—even a little?" I didn't add that I wanted to meet Libby, because I wasn't sure I did.

She shook her head, eyes blinking rapidly. To fight tears? "What I want," she said, "doesn't matter now. It didn't matter back then either."

Okay, then, the door was open.

"I couldn't handle it," I said, shocked at how whiny my voice sounded. "I couldn't deal with the Holocaust the way you could. I couldn't stand talking about it. I'm not like Simon, I couldn't stand being surrounded by it. It made me ashamed."

"But you're a child of a Holocaust survivor."

"That's it! That's exactly what I hate. It was exploding back in the 70s, the Holocaust was everywhere—in the news, magazines, TV shows, books coming out all the time, people talking about curricula in the schools." And the subject lived out in the open in Valerie's home and lurked in ours, but I didn't need to say that. "It made me sick. All those Jews marching off to death, standing there naked, being shot at the edge of pits, one-by-one. Those stick figures staring at the camera from behind barbed wire. The crematoriums. The piles of corpses. Whenever I looked at one of those photographs or saw film from when the Allies discovered the camps, I thought, 'That's not me, that can't be me. I'm not a victim.' So I ran away. I didn't want to be trapped by it."

"But you *are* trapped by it. Do you ever read about the camps? I didn't think so. Did you see *Schindler's List* or *Life is Beautiful* or *Shoah*? If you went to Amsterdam, you'd avoid Anne Frank's house, right? Then you're worse off now than before. You can't let it go."

"And you have?" I asked truculently.

"In a way. For years I used to think that was the most important thing in my life, what most identified me. I joined a therapy group here of children of survivors, and an international organization, the whole deal. But by the time I finished writing my memoir, I realized it wasn't everything about me. I'm comfortable with that part of my life, but it's sure not what makes me who I am or even makes me Jewish. And it didn't determine everything at home growing up—" She was speaking with more emphasis now. "My parents exhibit behavior lots of immigrants do, dislocation, fear, clinging to their kids, all of that. I've read enough and thought about it enough to see it clearly, and to—"

"To let go?" I asked, quoting her a little belligerently, but she didn't take any offense.

"To deal with it, to embrace it, to put it in perspective."

It sounded so much like the rap of a PBS fund drive psychological charlatan that my jaw stiffened. I felt the urge to push her away by saying something dismissive, yet there was her wavy red hair and her soft, sympathetic eyes that fought my defensiveness, and disarmed it.

I backed off, and just as our tuna came, I asked. "What's your new book about?"

She relaxed. Her shoulders had grown visibly tight and had started to rise up as if she were driving in bumper-to-bumper traffic, but now they sank back to normal. "I'm not really sure yet. I want to interview survivors to find out how they adjusted to life after the war, but I don't have a clear focus right now, and I haven't even done a proposal for my agent."

She had an agent, I thought, feeling shut out. But why was I surprised? She'd have everything you would associate with a real career. And she had a family, a daughter. I had, what was the word Mrs. Gordon had used? *Bubkes.* I had beans. A veritable hill of beans.

Valerie had grown up, and I hadn't.

"I'm hoping to find my theme in the interviews. It's not very organized, but—"

"Have you interviewed Mrs. Gordon?"

"I'm just breaking the ice with her. Sometimes it's slow, people don't want to talk, but they also don't *not* want to talk." She shook her head and smiled at the clumsy syntax. "They need to feel safe, and ready."

"Did you ever try getting my mother to talk to you about the War?"

She gave me a pitying look, but didn't brush off the question. "It never worked."

"You saw her a lot. Do you think she was depressed?"

Holding her fork over her plate, Val hesitated, as if weighing the meaning of that word. "Your Mom was never Betty Crocker."

"I know that, and I also know she wasn't taking anti-depressants, but her doctor said he recommended them to her. So he must have seen some kind of change. Was she worse than she used to be?" Asking her, I could almost feel the weight of my mother's occasional brooding silences, the way she could sit at the kitchen table ostensibly reading the newspaper but radiating a kind of dark helplessness, as if she were being swept into a maelstrom.

Val thought it over. "Your mother liked reading my reviews. I clipped them for her. But she couldn't read my memoir, and something changed after it was published. She was proud of me, she said so, but I felt, oh, more distance between us after the book came out." Val shifted uncomfortably in her seat, and her eyes clouded. "When I explained to her about the new book, and that I was going to interview Mrs. Gordon, who I met down in the lobby talking to your Mom—" she didn't go on.

"Tell me," I said.

Val leaned back from her dinner. She sighed, clasping and unclasping her hands. "I got the feeling she thought I was betraying her. That I was getting too close, almost forcing her to think about the War, to remember."

Then she swept a hand across her face with the quick gesture you'd use to brush off cobwebs you'd stumbled into. "Your mother went through a lot, more than we'll ever know. When your Dad got sick, it must have brought back the same sense of terror. I'm just guessing here, but it makes sense to me. She was losing everything again. I can't imagine watching someone you've been married to drift out to sea like that, day after day, and you can't stop it, can't call them back, and can't dive in after them. There's no rescue."

Val seemed tearful now and I wanted to get up, sit at her side and hold her. But I was afraid she'd think I was taking advantage of the moment, so I didn't move. I just poured both of us another glass of wine as I saw our waitress headed over to do just that and see how we were. I waved her off.

Without looking at me, and in a very low voice, Valerie went on, "I know this is crazy, but when your mother died, I felt kind of guilty. What if my talking about the War—even though it wasn't a lot, not a lot, really—what if that was bad for her heart? Maybe it was just one more thing that wore her down."

"You think what you were doing helped kill her?" I wanted to laugh because it was so outrageous. My mother couldn't have been that sensitive, that open to anyone's influence, not even Valerie's, though she seemed to have cared for Val more in life than for any of her own children. I hadn't been able to keep the surprise from my voice, and Valerie bristled at it.

She shot back: "When you've suffered the way she did, how can anyone predict what has an impact and what doesn't?"

"But your parents are fine, aren't they? Your writing hasn't hurt them, has it?"

She leaned forward, enunciating as clearly as if I needed to read her lips. "They—can—talk—about—it. Your mother kept everything inside. Even your Dad said that once. He had no idea what your Mom went through. She refused to tell him anything."

Even to Dad. This amazed me. What she'd suffered had been

so terrible it could never be expressed even to the man she'd been married to for over fifty years. To shape the obscenity in words was impossible. What could be so unimaginably terrible? Hundreds of people, thousands, had talked about the camps, written about them, been interviewed on film.

But then Val surprised me. "You know, your Mom was also getting forgetful. She used to tell me that she was afraid she'd end up like your father. I didn't see it, but maybe she was really alert to the smallest change because the signs would have been familiar."

We faced each other across the dreadful scenario of my mother not having died of a heart attack, but declining into incoherence like Dad, lurching from one loss of connection to another, until the woman she had been flickered and then went out, leaving a vacancy in the shape of a human being.

"The way she went was better," I said reluctantly. But then I thought of how people talked about sudden death, calling it merciful or lucky or easy. All of those labels were crude.

"If I ever start to lose it like Dad, I'd kill myself. I won't wait."

Val didn't flinch. "How would you do it?"

I picked an answer out of the air, but as soon as I said it, I sensed its perfect fit. "I'd drive out onto the highway, floor it, and smash into the back of a truck."

"That's a waste of a good car, isn't it?"

I started laughing, despite myself. After fifteen years, I was having dinner with Valerie, who was even more lustrously beautiful than before, and I was flinging around images of death, flames, dismemberment. And she could still make me laugh.

"You're right! I just got a new Grand Prix—it's terrific!" As I raved about the car, I imagined the two of us in it, speeding up north from Ann Arbor, the sun roof open, Val's hair fluttering around her head. Would Libby be there? I couldn't picture anything other than a midget version of Val.

Val saw that she had me on a roll, and she didn't let up. "Remember that joke in *Playboy* we loved about the woman who told a girlfriend she was all excited about going to the Grand Prix and the friend said, 'Honey, first thing you should know is you're pronouncing it wrong.'"

In the old days, I could be dark and despairing, riffing an emotional version of *Inna-Gadda-Da-Vida* and she'd undercut it with something, a remark, or a goofy face, hitting my gloom with the sunniness of Dr. Buzzard's Savannah Band.

"You always could figure out how to lighten me up," I marveled, wanting her to know I appreciated it.

"Monsieur," she said in a passable French accent, "Some things, they do not change." Her punctuating Gallic shrug was lovely, but I was suddenly hypersensitive again, wondering if she meant to be critical in saying "some things."

And a comment she'd made before we were laughing suggested a question I had to ask. "Did my mother ever talk about suicide?"

Valerie nodded reluctantly. "She followed that doctor in your state. The one who used to do mercy killings. Jack Kevorkian?"

"Dr. Death."

"Is that what they called him?"

I nodded and we told our waitress yes to coffee but no to dessert. She took away our dinners which I doubted either one of us had tasted.

"We used to talk about him a lot," Val said.

I was envious. The few times a year at most when I spoke with my mother on the phone, we had exchanged platitudes.

"She thought he was a hero, and hated that he was being prosecuted." Val looked so distracted, so open, I reached across the table and grabbed both her hands. She didn't pull away. They were very warm, and I was flooded with the memories of sleeping next to her, how warm and fragrant her body had been, how wonderful it was to fit against her full round ass and wake up in the middle of the night, one hand having slid down to her crotch, and my cock pressing apart her legs.

Her eyes widened, as if she were picturing exactly what I was. I didn't have to say it, but I did.

"I need you."

She shook her head and slid her hands out from mine.

"Valerie, don't you remember how good it was?" I hadn't been her first lover, but soon into sleeping together, she had told me that our sex was the way James Baldwin described it in *Another Country*, one of those long slow train rides.

"I never forgot."

"So? Last night you said I was desperate. I'm not. Not now. I love you."

She seemed not to hear that, and seemed deeply disturbed about something. "The timing's wrong. Talking about your Mom and dying and your Dad is really upsetting."

"Then why not—"

"Because I don't want to make love to forget." She withdrew her hands, put them in her lap a little primly.

"How does that add up?" I asked. It was obvious we weren't going to bed if we were starting to squabble about it, but I couldn't stop myself from plunging off this particular cliff.

The coffee came but neither one of us reached for our cups.

"Can't we talk about something else?" she asked.

"There is nothing else, not right now."

"You're unbelievable. You're just as arrogant as Dina is."

"Bullshit."

"Absolutely. Maybe even worse than Dina. No wonder you two never got along."

"Now you're my therapist?"

"Therapy wouldn't hurt you. Maybe you'd stop running so much."

"Running from what?" I asked perversely, almost wanting her to dump on me, wanting her anger. It was some kind of connection at least, not as hot as sex, but electric just the same.

"Is there anything you haven't run from? Me, your family, your past, your home, a real life. You should have seen your face when I mentioned Libby. You looked petrified. Hell, you're even running from an inheritance. How crazy is that?"

She pulled some bills from her wallet, struggled into her jacket, and said, "You're not a kid any more, but you still don't know what the hell you want."

"I want you!" I hissed, vainly trying to defuse the scene, aware that we were drawing prying looks from other diners. "Don't go."

But she did, and I thought I'd surely lost her for good.

• • • • •

In the cab up to Mom's apartment, I mused how mysterious Val's life had suddenly become. She had a daughter in—what?—first grade, second grade? Who was Libby named after? What kind of kid was she? How did she and Val interact? I couldn't see any of it. And Val would have a world of connections with other parents or single mothers that was totally alien to me.

But then I wondered if Valerie could be more drawn to me than I hoped, maybe still in love with me. Maybe she was protecting herself as much as Libby by keeping her daughter away, keeping her from making a connection between us.

Then I forgot about Libby. I asked the driver to turn the radio off because odd moments and comments at dinner had started to crystallize for me. Val wanted me to go back to Michigan, to stop asking questions. Val and my mother had talked about assisted suicide. My mother's doctor said she was depressed and he, too, had brushed me off. And Val had looked very troubled talking about Jack Kevorkian.

Everyone was telling me to go home, to stop asking questions.

Hadn't I sensed there was something wrong, without being able to pinpoint it? What if my mother had felt sure she was in the first stages of dementia and had committed suicide? With Val's help, or Mrs. Gordon's, the doctor's, or all of them? They all wanted me to drop the questions, to move on or even go home—why?

The cab stunk of pine-scented air freshener, making me wonder if someone had puked in it recently, and something vibrated in the door like a drill, so that by the time we hit the West Side Highway I had a headache. Every now and then something loomed up at me with bleak significance: the heliport making me wish for escape; the aircraft carrier docked at the Intrepid Sea and Flight M9useum, which left me feeling dwarfed and weak; the garbage barges at the Department of Sanitation, perfectly symbolizing where I was.

Back at the apartment, I called Simon right away and poured out all my suspicions.

"Are you high?" he asked carefully.

"No!"

"None of it adds up, Paul. So Dr. Stein was rude to you. He's busy, and you're not a patient of his anymore. Assisted suicide is illegal."

"It happens all the time anyway, and not just in Michigan."

Simon spoke more firmly than usual, as if to snap me out of a dizzy spell. "If Mom killed herself, it's none of our business." He went on to say that it was her choice to leave us and leave a husband who didn't recognize her anymore. "Could you blame her?"

I couldn't sleep that night. I combed through her medicine cabinet to see if I could find anything she might have taken, but I had only the vaguest ideas about what kind of pills could kill you, and gave up anyway when I realized that my mother was intelligent enough to have covered her tracks. The bequest felt even more painful, when I considered the ugly possibility of my mother's suicide, of her having brought on her death and my inheritance sooner.

I lay there in bed furiously jerking off in the hope it would tranquilize me, imagining Camilla riding me, but I kept thinking of Val. I'd ruined my chances with her by pushing her too hard to have sex, and then pushing her away when she said no. Dina was right, I was an asshole, I thought, as I burst like a geyser and fell asleep with my hands around my cock.

The phone woke me up and I staggered to it out in the kitchen. My mother's lawyer was calling me back, and he was either on a commuter train or somewhere in traffic. I asked him if she had ever explained anything about the German money and why she was leaving it to me.

"Nope. Never. I just drew up the new Will after your father got sick, according to her instructions."

His tone was dismissive and brusque. Once again, I was chilled by the New York rudeness I'd forgotten after my years in Michigan.

"What's the problem?" he asked after I didn't comment.

"It bothers me not to know why she left me all this money."

"Are you saying you don't want a million dollars—you got a *problem* with a million dollars?" He laughed scornfully and I thanked him for his time. Another dead end. Nothing was going to put my mind at rest.

I showered and made myself scrambled eggs in one of my mother's old cast iron fry pans, gulping orange juice from the container as if I'd been crawling across a desert. Our mother hated when we didn't use a glass and it felt good to defy even the memory of her disapproval. Standing there at the stove and eating the eggs out of the pan, I imagined calling Mom's doctor back and asking if she had committed suicide. He'd tell me I was nuts and probably threaten to sue me. There was no point in calling him.

But I could ask Mrs. Gordon. I was suddenly convinced that

she knew more about my mother than she'd been telling me.

"Another surprise!" she said a few minutes later when she let me in. "Wonderful!" I declined her offer of chocolate *babka*, but I accepted some coffee and we were soon in that overdone living room that was like a museum exhibit, in the same seats as yesterday.

"Your sister called me last night," she said from her chair. "Not too late."

"Dina called you? Why?"

"She wanted me to convince you to share your mother's money that came from Germany."

"What?"

Mrs. Gordon hushed me. "*Shah, shah*. Don't make such a *tsimmes* from it."

I was outraged and embarrassed, but Mrs. Gordon seemed amused.

"What did you tell her?"

"I got rid of her easy as pie." She wiped her hands on each other with satisfaction. "I agreed with every little thing she said. With a girl like this, you don't get nowhere by arguing. You say, Yes, darling, you're right, and she feels better and stops *hocking* you a *tchynick*."

I translated the Yiddish for myself: making a fuss. "That was smart," I said.

"Listen, Dina told me a little once about this husband of hers and his family, so I feel sorry for her."

Of course she could be sympathetic to Dina, she was an outsider and neutral. I doubted whether Dina had been even that open with our mother about Serge. She would have been afraid of a leaden "I told you so" or some other indictment. Dina hated to be wrong.

"How was your dinner with Valerie?" Mrs. Gordon asked brightly. "Such a lovely girl. She told me she was going out with you. She was very excited."

Val had been excited, and I'd completely pissed her off.

"Not well," I said, rising to go. Mrs. Gordon struggled up with her cane, but I told her I'd let myself out.

"I'll bring you up some *babka* later," I heard her call thinly from her chair as I let myself out into the hall and dragged my sorry butt up the stairs. What a loser. I had been right to speculate about Val's renewed interest in me, but what had I done? I obsessed about the German money and my mother's death. Cheerful conversation, guaranteed to make any woman fall into your arms, especially after a long absence.

How could I have been so misguided? Why didn't I buy her flowers? Or surprise her by arriving at her apartment with a bottle of champagne? No, that would have been showy and excessive, just like pushing her to come home with me. I'd hoped that being together would spark something in her. If it had, I'd doused it with my stupidity.

And now I was even suspecting her of helping my mother commit suicide. From lover to killer—it had the earmarks of a movie on the Lifetime channel.

Wasn't it time to give up and go back to what I called my life in Michigan?

Simon had left me a message while I was at Mrs. Gordon's: "Dina flew down from Quebec. I'm picking her up at the airport and we're coming over around noon. She didn't tell me what's up."

More melodrama, probably.

I went out to Broadway to buy a *New York Times*, which was thicker than the national edition I sometimes read. But on the way back, I remembered my mother's keys and stopped at Mrs. Gordon's.

"Keys?" she asked vaguely, holding the door open and peering up at me as if I were a stranger. "What keys?"

"The set of keys my mother gave you for emergencies."

She squinted hard, as if trying to make them appear in the air between us. "You know, doll, I'm not so sure where I put them, but I'll look." She smiled as if she'd actually found them, and I thanked her.

By the time I was done with the paper upstairs, Simon and Dina showed up. She was in a royal blue power suit and pumps, and her face was so tight she looked like she had a gun in the Chanel bag she was itching to use on me. I was angry, too, at both of them for never telling me that Valerie had a daughter. It was their fault, wasn't it, that I'd been surprised at dinner, waylaid.

I wanted to say something mean to Dina like, "To what do I owe the pleasure of this visit?" but I settled for hello and just followed her into the living room. Simon met my eyes and shrugged.

Dina parked her angry self on a window seat as if she were a judge opening up a trial. Simon and I sat on the couch and waited.

"I've thought this over, Paul. I've talked to Serge, and to our lawyer. It's very simple. If you don't divide the German money three ways, I'm going to contest the Will."

Simon went pale.

"That'll tie up the estate for a very long time," she said with savage exactness, "and I'm sure you can't afford a legal battle."

I was speechless, but Simon wasn't. Rather than try to mediate, as he'd always done before, he burst out: "You're unreasonable, Dina. I'll sell the co-op and split the money with you—I told you that already."

She shook her head, lips tight, and I could see the excitement in her eyes, could imagine the way she had armed herself to fly down here and do battle with me.

"What grounds?" I asked. "You have to have grounds to contest a Will."

"Mom was starting to forget things. She probably had Alzheimer's." Dina said it so combatively that I wondered if I'd been wrong assuming the same thing. I couldn't imagine Dina was right; she was just using the disease as a weapon, as an excuse.

"What is your problem?" I asked.

"You're my problem. You're not really part of the family, so why should you be treated as special? Because you sent Mom some birthday cards when you forgot to leave a message on her machine? On the machine! You couldn't be bothered to talk to her directly. You abandoned her and Dad and us and now you're waltzing away with everything? No. It's not going to happen." Her lips quivered.

"You've been off in Boston and Montreal for years," I shouted. "How's that any better? You married a Catholic! In a church!" I didn't care, but I had to throw something back at her. This, I thought, was how violence erupted in families. I felt my whole body tensed for an assault.

Simon grabbed my arm to quiet me down, but I was shocked when he told Dina, "Leave Paul alone."

She stared evilly at him, then me. "You've been plotting against me, haven't you?"

Of course we both said "No" at the same time.

Dina stomped out to the foyer, and we were sucked along in her wake. Turning at the door, she said to me, "Now I know why you never married Val and never settled down. You're probably bisexual, too." She waved at me and Simon. "And this is very, very sick."

She was out the door before it fully registered on me what she was implying, and I doubled up in laughter, letting go all the tension of the last few days so wildly that I was soon leaning against the foyer wall to steady myself. Simon seemed almost worried.

"Weren't you taking her back to the airport?" I asked.

"She said she was going shopping on Madison."

"God, can't you just see her date book for today? 'New York: Berate Simon and Paul; Buy Shoes.'"

Now it was Simon's turn to lose it, and I watched him let go. When he'd laughed himself out, I hugged him, thinking how strange it was that our mother's death should have brought us closer while it opened up a crevasse between me and Dina. If nothing else had come out of my time in New York, there was this growing connection with him. I ruffled his hair and he said "Stop!" just like when we were kids.

"If Dina wants to have the Will contested," I said as he left, "I don't care. I'm so confused about the money there's no rush to have it."

"She won't," he predicted. "She's just trying to scare you. She's a bully."

"I may leave tomorrow, so should I just drop my keys with the super?"

Simon nodded and said, "Call me when you get back to Michigan."

There was no doubt that I would.

Keys, I thought a little while later. I should go down and ask Mrs. Gordon if she needed help finding the extra set of my mother's keys.

Downstairs, Mrs. Gordon blithely said she hadn't found them yet. "My head." She pointed to her forehead, sounding like a fond dog owner excusing her pet's mess.

Somehow, though, I didn't believe her. I'd only known her a few days, but she had always seemed sharp before.

"How about some of your *babka*?" I asked, partly because I sensed her reluctance to let me in. I followed her into the kitchen, helped her serve slices for each of us.

"Milk?" she asked a bit too politely.

"Great." I poured myself a tumbler full and ferried the food out into the living room while she proceeded with her cane, walking slowly and unsteadily.

She frowned and looked around the crowded room. "I wish I could remember where I put them."

"I could help you look."

"Noooo. . . . You don't want to be going through an old lady's things."

"I've gone through my mother's," I offered.

"*Nu*? So why aren't you trying the cake? All of a sudden you're shy?"

I spread the thick linen napkin on my lap, set the cake plate down and cut a piece with my heavy silver fork. It was as delicious as everything else she'd baked, flaky and filled with chocolate and raisins, perfectly complimented by the milk.

"Good, good," she said.

"When did my mother give you the set of keys?"

Mrs. Gordon shrugged. "Who can remember?"

"But you haven't lived here that long."

"When you get to be my age, you'll know that what happened yesterday you can't remember, but years ago, that's like diamonds it's so sharp."

I decided to drop it, not even sure why I was hassling her about the keys. There was something more important to raise with Mrs. Gordon.

"I'm going home tomorrow. But before I leave I want to ask you something."

Her hands froze in her lap, and I had the weird sense she was watching my every move as if I were dangerous.

"I've been wondering about how my mother died."

She raised her eyebrows attentively. "Yes?"

"No history of heart trouble. She walked every day. But she was depressed. Her doctor said so. Valerie said so. I'm not sure how, but I think one of them might have helped her commit suicide because she was starting to forget things and she was afraid she'd end up like Dad. Maybe they both helped her, I don't know, and I'm beginning not to care. She's dead no matter how it happened."

"Yes," Mrs. Gordon said flatly, "she's dead."

I thought of having told Valerie I'd drive into a truck to kill myself. That seemed like pure bravado. "I don't think I'd have her courage."

"*Courage?*" Mrs. Gordon's cup rattled a little in the saucer.

"To kill myself. Even with help, it would be hard to do."

Mrs. Gordon's face crumpled up as if she were about to spit something out. "Valerie didn't have nothing to do with it," she snapped, her voice thin. "Not the doctor neither. Your mother wasn't no hero. She didn't commit suicide. She just died, that's all."

Starting to choke up, I said, "But I feel guilty. I wasn't a good son. She deserved more."

"*Bubbeh mysehs!* Nonsense. You don't know nothing about what she deserved."

Her bitter tone confused me. "Did she tell you something about the War?"

"Hah! You must be joking! It's not what she said that told me."

I set my cake plate aside, discarded the cloth napkin.

Mrs. Gordon's lips were trembling and she held her hands as if to keep them from shaking. "First time I met your mother, I said '*Foon vanent koomt a Yeed?*' Where are you from? She acted hoity-toity. She said by her at home they didn't speak Yiddish— just Russian and Polish." Mrs. Gordon shrugged. "Fine. Lots of Jews, they made fun of Yiddish, they called it *jargon*. So, I asked where she was from. With her accent, I figured she was a Litvak. And she said near Vilna. Lots of Jews tell you this, they want to show off they're close to the big city even if they're not. A little exaggeration doesn't hurt. This, it didn't bother me."

I had no idea what she was talking about, and wondered if Mrs. Gordon's mind was wandering. It sounded sensible, but didn't mean anything.

"So I ask her 'Where?' She tells me it's a nothing town, what we call a *lochovich lochovitchki*, a real little hole. Balbirishok.

Then I ask her family name, she tells me Amdursky. I don't say anything. I go home, I sit and I think. I think for a long, long time."

"About what? What did she say that bothered you?"

Eyes narrowed, she leaned forward from her chair, gripping the handle of her cane so tightly her knuckles were white. "You want to know what bothered me? I'll tell you. Balbirishok? I had family there! Cousins. I been there before the war and never seen your mother." She nodded fiercely. "But that's not everything. Her name's Rose Amdursky? From Balbirishok? *Impossible!* I was in the Vilna ghetto with Rose Amdursky—and the camp in Riga—and then Stutthoff—then Magdeburg. She was my best friend in the ghetto. And I seen her die with my own eyes, almost at the end of the War. Typhus."

"It must be somebody else."

Mrs. Gordon glared at me. "I'd swear this in a court. You think there were hundreds of Rose Amdursky's from Balbirishok? There wasn't hardly hundreds of Jews!"

Stunned, I asked her what she was trying to tell me.

"Whoever your mother was, she was *not* Rose Amdursky. This I know for sure. I don't know how she came to steal this name, but hers, it's not. Listen to me, Rose saved my life in one camp. I was sick, we had no food, they were starving us, beating us, waiting for us to die. Somehow, Rose, she got me a piece cheese. That's all it took to make a difference! You think I would forget anything about such a woman?"

"But why would my mother pretend to be somebody else? "

"Exactly. Why? This is what I asked myself. And I figured, you take somebody else's name, you have something you're running away from. Your own name is trouble, who you *are* is trouble. So why should this be for your mother?"

I listened to her, but the words seemed to circle my head without penetrating.

"So. Your mother had something to hide."

"What?"

"You know, at the end of the War, with the Russians coming from the East, the Nazis and their *farsholteneh* assistants, the damned henchmen—Poles, Lithuanians, Ukrainians—they were all running like rabbits, but still killing, shooting anyone they could, burning. Some threw off their uniforms. Some put on camp clothes to be disguised. Most of them, they was caught, someone recognized them, but not all."

"No."

She shrugged.

Dazed, nauseous, I asked her if she was saying my mother was some kind of a war criminal.

She replied in a sepulchral voice, "What else could she be if she lied about where she came from, who she was? A Jew would pretend to be another Jew? *Narishkeit!* What for?"

"You don't know that! You don't have any proof!" But even as I said it, I felt ripped open by the possibility. It meant that my mother's long angry silence about the War wasn't trauma, it was *terror*.

"I have the proof of what I saw, what I lived through. I didn't need nothing more."

My mother must have been afraid someone would discover who she was. And somebody had. "You killed her," I said in that madly crowded and overstuffed room. I waited for Mrs. Gordon to deny my charge, to tell me I was hysterical, anything. She stared me down, as hard-eyed as Dina could be.

"I don't know who she was exactly, I figured some kind of guard, a Lithuanian, a Pole, a *blockowa*, the criminals they put in charge of the barracks. Not a Jew. Why would a Jew want to hide? Someone maybe who was around Jews in her life, and thought she could pretend."

"No."

"Okay, maybe she was a Jew, a collaborator, somebody helping the Nazis to save her own life. But whoever it was—"

"How?"

"My heart medicine. I crushed the pills and baked for her a marble cake. Your mother loved my marble cake."

Jolted, I turned to my plate.

"Please," she said. "You think I'm a monster? I got nothing against you."

"How could you be sure it would work?"

"I read about it in a book, one of your mother's mysteries I borrowed gave me the idea."

"Why didn't you ask her what happened? Why didn't you try to find out who she really was?"

"Why, why, why. You think she does something so desperate, she takes somebody else's name and identity, lives a whole life like that, then she's going to confess—boom!—just because I say, 'Excuse me, so who are you exactly?'"

"You could have gone to the police."

"And they would listen to a crazy old lady? No. This was what I had to do, for my friend. For my Rose. Not for anybody else. Rose Amdursky saved my life, and now I was going to let somebody else steal hers? And get away with it like nobody's business? Never."

Horrified, I tried to find some hope in the middle of this brutal nightmare, but I was like those people in "Titanic" clinging wildly to railings as the ship tipped over and dropped them into the icy North Atlantic. Nothing could stop the plunge.

"But if she was a fraud, how did she get the German money? Didn't she have to have witnesses or something? I'm sure there were people who had to swear to her identity."

"You know these witnesses, where they came from, what they did? You ever met them?"

I shook my head.

"I couldn't wait for somebody else to find out. It was so many years later. And what if something happened to me? Then nobody would know and she would get away with everything."

I managed to say, "You told her you knew?"

"*A voo den*? Of course! I should let her die in peace? She didn't feel so well, I helped her lie down, then, I told her when she couldn't do nothing. I did this for Rose Amdursky, the real one, my Rose. I owed her."

I sat there with the weight of Mrs. Gordon's revelations crushing me like a landslide. I could feel my lungs go tight, each breath an effort.

"Why did you tell me?"

She wagged a bony finger at me. "That woman left you the German money which she stole from the *real* Rose Amdursky. So you should know the *real* story, or what's more real than the lies. It's what I can leave you with."

"Leave me with the truth? You're sick? Are you dying?"

She smiled ruefully. "That would be the easy way out, huh? No, darling, I may have to live a long time with what I did."

"What did she say?"

"When she was dying?" Mrs. Gordon shook her head. "*Gornisht*. Not one word. But her eyes, before they was closed, I'm telling you, *that* was some look she was giving me."

"You watched her die?"

Mrs. Gordon nodded.

Utterly shattered, I made myself stand and walk to the door, every detail of which was hideous and unreal. But once out in the hallway, I couldn't imagine doing anything as ordinary as ringing the buzzer for the elevator, and the thought of having to even look at another person left me feeling burned and raw. I staggered over to the stairs, climbed a few and then sat down, the worn marble startling, cold, and hard underneath me. Grimy light filtered through the huge opaque window and my breathing was becoming more painful. I wanted to die. I thought of yanking up the window and hurling myself into the air shaft but I wasn't high enough, just a few floors up. I pictured stepping out onto the street in front of a car. Each vision left me mangled, bleeding, but not dead, not dead. And would killing myself even matter? This was a horror that would transcend death, pursuing me into any other world.

No, that was crazy. I wanted to live, and to leave. I found myself aching to be home in Michigan right then, away from little old ladies telling stories of murder and revenge while they served you dessert.

But would I ever have a home anywhere now? My mother had been a Nazi, or a Nazi sympathizer, or had helped them, someone involved with the camps. What else could it be? What else would make her steal another woman's name? No wonder she hated Simon reading about the Holocaust, and walked away when people talked about it, and fought Dad's push to apply for reparations. She risked getting found out. But how had she located people willing to swear she was someone she wasn't? Who were they—where did they come from?

Her blood, her evil, was part of me, ineradicable. And how could I live the rest of my life knowing, or just suspecting, that my mother had persecuted Jews? And not only wasn't she who she said she was, she might not even have been Jewish, which would mean that technically, I wasn't either.

Mrs. Gordon's truth-telling had gouged chunks out of my life as violently as some madman taking a hammer to a famed sculpture. I shuddered. My mother had been murdered. I had sat there with a killer. A soft-spoken, white-haired charming killer in a fucking nylon track suit looking like thousands of women her age.

I heard steps below. Someone was walking upstairs and I blindly hurried away to Mom's apartment, feeling like Hercules wearing the poisoned shirt that burned his flesh.

I went straight to the bottle of Scotch I'd found and downed half of what was there, letting it sear my throat. I tried calling Valerie, but hung up when I got her machine. There was nothing I could imagine saying to her tape, not yet.

What should I do? Call the police? Would they believe me if Mrs. Gordon denied it. Would they exhume my mother's body? It was hideous, unbelievable, and I reeled through the apartment wanting to scream, to tear Mrs. Gordon's words from my brain.

Think, think, I commanded myself, but I couldn't. I felt like a medieval prisoner with his limbs tied to four horses. If I stayed a moment longer I'd be ripped apart. I threw my clothes and toiletries in my bag, sealed the bottle of scotch, cleaned up in the kitchen as well as I could, and got ready to flee the apartment I hoped never to see again. But before I left, I went to my mother's machine and erased her greeting. I didn't know when Simon might change it, but I never wanted to hear her voice again. I recorded a quick message of my own. I took the keys with me, deciding to send them to Simon from Michigan, locked up, and I raced down the stairs to find a cab out on West End Avenue that would take me to La Guardia.

At the airport, I slowed down. I had to. There was a massive line at the Northwest counter, and oddly, in the midst of the crowd, I could think. After changing my flight, I called Simon and explained about the keys, and I thanked him for being a wonderful brother. The words came with difficulty, and when I hung up I thought he might find them corny or stiff, but I had to start somewhere.

And then I called Valerie and didn't hang up when her tape came on.

"Val, can you forgive me? I pushed too hard because I love you. I've always loved you. The worst mistake of my life was leaving New York and leaving you. Is it too late? Will you marry me?"

A thirtyish Chicano security guard in a lumpy uniform nearby turned at my question and grinned, giving me a thumb's up.

• • • • •

Back in Ann Arbor, I begged for a few more days off, looking as ravaged and desperate as a fugitive from justice, no doubt, and sped north to Old Mission which I reached late at night. In my co-worker's cabin, I called Valerie to leave my number. Then I called back three times, then four, remembering the awful scene in *Swingers* where John Favreau destroys his chances of a relationship by his paranoid neediness, but I couldn't control myself. I needed to hear her voice, and a taped message would do for a little while. In various bumbling ways I said it was me calling each time, and that I loved her.

Each time I said it, I was fighting the horror of my mother's death, lying there betrayed by her friend, quietly gloated over, helpless. I didn't know who she really was or what she'd done, but I felt lost in her helplessness at the end. My proud, strong mother brought low by a little old lady's marble cake.

And the cabin felt like a prison, too. I felt reckless and stupid. I hadn't made a plan. What was I going to do? At La Guardia, I'd wanted to return to Old Mission the way romantic, lonely people say they'd like to see Venice some day, but I was *here*, barely had touched ground at my apartment in Ann Arbor, which looked obscenely pristine, as untouched by disaster as that one house or silo that seems to evade the tornado's wrath and pokes up from the middle of acres of rubble. I was up north again, but now what?

It was suddenly hard to recapture my contentment, my vision of Old Mission. I wanted to strip away complexity and pain, but I felt hemmed in. I flung myself out of the cabin into the darkness, stumbling down the hill to the vast blue bay. I ripped off my sweats and running shoes, burst into the frigid water, my feet grabbed by rocks, splashing, desperate. I swam with fury in each stabbing arm until I felt drained, out, out into the bay and then back, slowly but desperately when I thought I was on the edge of losing all power and feeling in my arms. I stumbled out of the water to fall on the cold sand, face up, gasping, the icy air sucking at my skin.

My mother was dead. She was very possibly a murderer, a war criminal. It could be nothing less that had made her steal an identity and hide behind it for decades.

There on my back on the star-silvered beach, eyes closed to block out the incredible bright sky, my mother's death and betrayal howled inside of me. I had not been close enough to Dad to truly begin missing him even though he'd been sick and absent for so long, but her, oh I had loved and hated her wildly in the silent extravagance of despair.

As my chest rode waves of pain, I felt scorched by the German money she had been forced to apply for and had left me. But why? What did she want me to remember, to think, to feel? Surely not this. I had nowhere to hide from these mysteries, not even Old Mission.

When I got back to the cabin I had to call Val. Libby answered, speaking as if she had been trained to be very clear and polite on the phone: "Hel-lo. Who's calling, please?"

I hesitated, and could hear Val in the background prompting her: "Honey, ask again."

"Hello? Who's calling?" Her voice was thin and delicate, and I suddenly pictured Simon answering the phone as a little boy, holding the huge receiver in both hands.

The phone clunked and Libby raised her voice, "Mommy, nobody's there!"

Val got on the line. "Who is this?" she asked warily.

"It's me!"

"Oh, Paul—why didn't you say so?" I heard a door close.

"I was startled. I didn't expect Libby to answer the phone." What an idiot I was—why hadn't I tried talking to Val's daughter?

"Well, she lives here, doesn't she?"

And would, I thought, for years to come. I had lost the chance of having Valerie to myself. I tried to think of something gracious to say, or something funny, but I came up blank.

"Paul, your message surprised me."

"The first message from La Guardia? When I asked you to marry me?"

"Yes, that's the one. What's going on? Why did you leave so fast?"

"It was time." Trying to keep my voice neutral but not cold, I said, "I was getting dragged down staying at my mother's."

"I can understand that." The bit of warmth in her voice brought me close to tears. She must have heard something in my silence because she said, "Are you okay?

"I fucked up. I really need to see you."

"Are you coming back?" She sounded dubious.

"I can't handle it right now. The apartment, Dina, everything. God, New York. Would you even consider flying out here?"

She breathed in slowly. "Well, I might be able to swing some free time for a visit. A short one."

"When? How about this weekend? Couldn't you ask your folks to take Libby?"

"This weekend? Whoa! They might have plans. Arranging child care isn't like checking a bag. It takes time, and mostly it's pretty frustrating."

"Well, if it did work, when would you know? Tomorrow?"

"I'd have to get right on it, whenever."

"Please. . . ."

"Okay. I'll try. No promises. But I'll try to see if I can get a ticket. And whenever I do come out there, could we talk a little less about death and your Mom this time?" she asked.

• • • • •

Val called me later that evening to say there were actually more seats available for that weekend than any other in the coming month. "I don't know why," she said, "But that's how it works out."

I tried not to crow.

When I went to bed, knowing that she was flying into Traverse City via Detroit the afternoon after next, I wondered what Val intended. Was she flying out simply to take a better look at me, to inspect me away from my family and New York and our past? Was it just morbid curiosity?

Despite my anxiety about Val, and my scene that morning with Mrs. Gordon, I knew I would sleep through the night just from exhaustion. I dreamt of my mother in her bed, Mrs. Gordon hovering over her like a vulture, the two of them locked in silent hatred.

In the morning I was able to book us one of the first-floor suites at Chateau Chantal, thanks to a lucky cancellation.

I arrived at the tiny Traverse City airport early on Friday with a bouquet of white and red carnations. I'd first considered roses, but the association with my mother was too awful.

Val showed up at the head of a line of fat, cranky-looking travelers, grinning at me and nodding at the flowers which she buried her nose in. People were staring at us, perhaps wondering why we weren't hugging, but I held back, not wanting to force myself on her in any way. There was too much at stake now. "Wonderful flowers. Like cinnamon," she breathed.

I offered to take her huge black shoulder bag, but she demurred.

"You look great," I said, and she seemed perfectly dressed for travel. In comfortable-looking black walking shoes, she wore a sage-colored quilted jacket and matching black and sage paisley dress.

"I wore the paisleys just for you and the warm jacket for Michigan."

As we headed for the uncrowded little parking lot, our typical banalities about her flight seemed charged with romance to me as I imagined meeting her like this for the rest of our lives, much of which would be spent talking about the simplest things. That was what I craved: simplicity, with her.

But she had Libby, and that was anything but simple.

Val walked around my bright blue Grand Prix and gave it a wolf whistle. "Wow," she said, and I felt suddenly defensive.

"You don't think it's too flashy or anything?"

"If I did, would you sell it?" I must have looked surprised, because she patted my shoulder. "Kidding! This is really hot."

I flushed with pleasure and opened the doors. Valerie slung her travel bag in the back seat but lay the flowers down like a sleeping child. As we headed off, I told her about the suite at Chateau Chantal, and that we could sleep in separate beds in separate rooms. I didn't care to rush anything.

"I just want to be near you. That's all."

She looked down, absorbing that remark. I studied her freckled cheek, her curly hair, the way her chiffon scarf seemed to float against her neck.

We took the scenic drive along the winding coast road, which I told her was 36 miles long.

"That's twice *chai*!" she exclaimed.

"What?"

"You know. *Chai* is Hebrew for 'life' and its numerical value when you add the letters up is 18."

"Oh, right." Simon had explained that to me before.

"Twice chai is very lucky."

I didn't resonate to this news, but her excitement made me tingle as much as if I'd built the damned road myself and ensured its exact distance.

Val kept praising the views of the water, the hills, the large and small houses tucked into woods or right on the shore, then laughed at her own delight. "It really is beautiful. I had no idea. When you say Michigan, I think of cars and Detroit. That's about it."

I told her that she would be amazed at Old Mission in May, when the cherry trees bloomed up and down the peninsula.

"It's like an enormous parade float. The Rose Bowl! Or a giant birthday cake with a billion candles."

Val took my hand, squeezed it. "What the hell are you doing in a library?" she asked. "You should be a writer or something."

"I should definitely be something."

Driving that afternoon on Old Mission I felt that each comment, each observation, each mile took us light years from the confusion and missed connections of our dinner three nights before. We chatted mostly about what we saw—the ever-changing view, brand-new Victorian-style homes, orchards—and the natural fluidity building between us was like strong hands massaging your neck and bringing relief to each tight and weary muscle.

"I made an early dinner reservation," I told her. "We could go right to the restaurant and check into the B&B later. It's not formal. That's the neat thing up here, you can eat at good restaurants but you don't have to dress up."

"Sounds great. I am hungry."

We pulled up to the Bowers Harbor Inn, an unexceptional-looking large white frame house with one of northern Michigan's best restaurants. We had the dark, lustrous dining room to ourselves for a while, and it was like being in someone's boudoir: intimate and relaxing. Valerie insisted on choosing the wine, and we had a plummy Gigondas with our duck sausage appetizer and rack of venison.

Sitting off in a well-curtained corner, all alone, we couldn't have found a more private place to talk, and the first thing Valerie told me was that Dina had called her.

"Dina's calling everyone," I snapped.

She frowned. "Who else?"

"Mrs. Gordon." I hoped my eyes weren't revealing anything at that moment.

"Well, Dina called to apologize for her fight with you and Simon. Not to apologize, I mean, that wasn't what she said she was calling for. But that's what it was. She was feeling really guilty."

"She should. She threatened to challenge my mother's Will because she wants a share of the German money."

Valerie set her fork down. "Okay—how much money are we talking about here?" I told her, and she was shocked. "A million dollars might make me a little crazy, too. But I wouldn't worry about Dina any more. She's thinking of divorcing Serge and she'll have lots of money eventually that she won't have to share with anyone."

I could not feel sorry for Dina, at least not yet. I could picture Mom shaking her head at the news, simmering with unspoken "I told you so's."

The wine disappeared and we ordered a second bottle, with Valerie seeming more and more relaxed. "I did probably talk about the Holocaust too much years ago, didn't I?" she asked.

I nodded, thankful for her graceful admission.

"I couldn't help myself," she noted. "But I needed to work it through back then, and that was just the beginning. Writing the memoir made the change."

"I'd like to read it," I said, "When you think I'm ready."

She nodded. "You know, I hated you for leaving," she said. "The first time. And I thought all that stuff about the Holocaust was bullshit, that it was really me, just me, you wanted to get away from."

"*No*—"

She cut me off with a wave of her hand. "I wanted to fuck you out of my system."

"Did you try?" I asked.

"I'm not the warrior maiden type—I let other people keep fighting the Sexual Revolution. Therapy saved me from becoming bitter. You still mean a lot to me. That hasn't changed."

"But *you* have. You have a daughter."

"Does it bother you—are you jealous? Of Steve?"

195

"No. I'm jealous of *you*. I moved away, but you moved ahead."

Val asked what I wanted to do with my inheritance, and when I answered, I knew I had resolved another uncertainty: "I want to buy a house up here."

"And quit your job?"

"Yes."

"What would you do? And would you live here year-round? The winters must be fierce."

I didn't answer and Val sipped some more wine before she said, "You should try Florida for part of the year. It's not bad, and at least it's warm. My parents keep offering to buy me a two-bedroom somewhere so I can have privacy when I visit them, and write."

Our eyes met in a question and I spoke first. "I'm not wild about New York, but I'd try living there, for you."

"We could try all three places—New York, Michigan *and* Florida—to start, anyway."

I asked, "Would it work?"

Val was tentative. "If we wanted it to. I can see myself writing a book up here, too. It's so peaceful."

"What about Libby—is she too young to deal with all this?"

"She's tough, and if we ended up moving here, I think she would adjust. But with kids, you never know." She smiled. "Libby asked me why you were calling me so many times and leaving so many messages. She asked if you were an actor, re-hearsing for a play." Val shook her head, enjoying the joke.

"Can I see her pictures?"

"Later. I brought an album. A small album." She shrugged.

I smiled. "An album's fine. Even a videotape. Did you tell Libby you were seeing me?"

"I said you were an old friend."

"Do you think she'd like me?"

"It's a good question. It's the big question. We'll have to find out."

"Has it been hard raising her by yourself?"

"Raising children is always hard. And exhilarating—beautiful—sad."

"Why sad?"

"Because just when you feel you know them or feel comfortable with who they are, they're leaving that stage behind. But that's life, isn't it?" She shrugged again.

Growing up, I had never imagined myself as a father, and even when Valerie and I were dating, children weren't on my mind. But she was different now, and I would have to grow up with her. It would not be a Hollywood romance, it would be work, and I had to give myself to it and to her completely.

We skipped dessert and coffee, and lurching to the car, I knew it was time to slip my arm around her.

"The sky is so bright," she marveled. "You can see the Milky Way." I felt as proud as if I'd ordered a mariachi band to serenade her.

I was pretty wasted, and drove very carefully back across the peninsula to Chateau Chantal. The narrow road up to the winery was long and winding, and for some reason the slow climb made us both silly. Letting ourselves in at the massive doors, we giggled helplessly and sped across the two-story hall down the corridor to our suite as if pulling a fast one on somebody.

Inside, I locked the door and moved to Valerie in our private living room, basking in her perfume and the wine on her breath as we kissed. We were trying to shuck off our clothes as we staggered against each other toward the bed, and I fumbled in my pocket for a condom. Val hauled back the expensive fitted green brocade bed spread, flinging the throw pillows around the room and laughing as she fell backwards with her arms up in the air, fingers wriggling, legs bare.

"We forgot your flowers in the car," I said.

"Don't you dare walk out on me now," she warned, sitting up bleary-eyed as if she were looking for something to hurl at me.

"Come here."

Obediently, I followed her orders and my hard-on to the bed. She yanked my pants open, held out her hand for the condom packet which she deftly unwrapped and popped into her mouth. As I quivered, she expertly, slowly unraveled the condom onto my cock, her mouth so warm I thought I'd shoot right then. When she finished, I fell on her hungrily and her legs crossed and uncrossed on my butt as she groaned. My head was buried in her neck, breathing in her sweat, her hair as if each inhalation would save me.

I was too thrilled to calculate my effects, to think of moves and transitions, to follow a blueprint. I simply held on to her as we see-sawed on the bed, with no sense of separation, no feeling that I was watching her and myself from any sort of distance.

After only a few sweaty minutes with her, I could feel Val's thighs trembling and knew that she was close to coming. I was desperate to hang on. Then she moaned "Oh, I love you. . . ." It was the ultimate turn-on, and I came with her. We lay there entangled and replete, breathing deeply.

"Just like one of the first times," she said drowsily. "Remember? We barely got our clothes off."

"I'm sorry it was so fast."

"Fast? It took fifteen years to get here. . . ."

I disengaged carefully, took off the condom while she struggled out of the rest of her clothes. I tucked her into bed, closing the lights around the room, and washed up briefly. Done, I was caught by my reflection in the large baroque mirror, suddenly aware how much I looked like my mother, even with my face flushed and relaxed.

"Where the hell are you?" Val called, half-asleep now as I turned off the bathroom light. I slipped into bed behind her, nestling against her warm back, soft butt and long legs, relishing the sensations that were as quietly dazzling as I'd remembered.

We were fifteen years older, but I felt like a horny happy kid again, in love with love, with her body and mine, and more: with all the possibilities that had unfolded in each kiss, each joke, each touch of her hand.

"You never said if you'd marry me or not," I whispered against her ear, the warmth of our bodies surrounding us as densely as the thicket around Sleeping Beauty's castle.

She muttered, "Be quiet—maybe—if everything works out for us."

I grinned, listening to her breathing slow down and grow deeper, steadier, hypnotic. I knew that if I followed that rhythm, I would be asleep very soon.

Before her confession, Mrs. Gordon had said that taking my mother's money would bring something good out of something terrible. That was truer now than before. I was going to buy myself a very small piece of Old Mission Peninsula with it. I would escape a job that was sterile and unappealing, to explore my future. I would get my courage up and do what I had longed to do as a boy: write. A book about Old Mission, about its hills and arbors and wine and shores.

It was not too late to rebuild my life—with Valerie and Libby. I thought of that line from Jodie Foster's *Contact*: "The only thing that makes the emptiness bearable is each other."

Then I pictured my mother dying with Mrs. Gordon's un-forgiving face the last thing she saw. Was she thinking of me, wishing I were there, or wondering how I'd feel about the Ger-many money? I could see her look of disgust when I'd broken up with Valerie, when I'd chosen a dead-end career. Maybe that was why she'd given me this inheritance—to liberate me from my mistakes. Surely the German money had burdened her, and maybe leaving it to me had freed her.

But I could never tell Val, or Simon and Dina, everything that Mrs. Gordon had revealed to me about my mother in what seemed now like another life, another world.

Lying there with Valerie in my arms at last, it was as clear as

the Milky Way to me that I had wasted too much of my life trying to escape the forces that had made me. I had finally stopped
running. I was ready for life, for Valerie, even to find my way as
a parent.

And ready to embrace a strange new reality.

Whatever the German money meant, I was truly my mother's
son.

I had a secret, too.

Acknowledgments

Thanks for their invaluable advice, encouragement, and assistance to Mary Bisbee, Linda Fairstein, Marilyn Hassid, Gershen Kaufman, Kristin Lauer, Anne Tracy & Ira Wood.

About the Author

Lev Raphael was born and raised in New York City, the son of Holocaust survivors. He did an MFA in Creative Writing at the University of Massachusetts at Amherst where he won the Harvey Swados Fiction Prize, awarded by Martha Foley for a story later published in *Redbook*.

He holds a Ph.D. in American Studies from Michigan State University, where he taught Creative Writing and many other courses. Raphael's short fiction and creative nonfiction have appeared in two dozen anthologies in the U.S. and Britain, most recently in *American Jewish Fiction: A Century of Stories*, which includes work by Saul Bellow, Cynthia Ozick, and Allegra Goodman.

One of America's earliest Second Generation writers, Raphael has published dozens of stories, essays, and articles in a wide range of newspapers, magazines and journals. His stories and essays are on college and university syllabi around the U.S. and in Canada. His fiction has also been analyzed in scholarly journals and at conferences like MLA in the U.S. and abroad. Raphael is a winner of Amelia's Reed Smith Fiction Prize and International Quarterly's Crossing Boundaries Prize for innovative prose, awarded by D.M. Thomas. That memoir appears in his collection of memoirs and essays *Journeys & Arrivals*. His first collection of short stories *Dancing on Tisha B'Av* won a 1990 Lambda Literary Award and has been in print ever since. Raphael is also the author of a literary novel, *Winter Eyes*, a scholarly book about Edith Wharton's life and fiction, and four co-authored books in psychology and education. He has also published five comic academic mysteries.

He has done well over 125 invited readings from his fiction

and nonfiction in North America, Europe, and Israel at colleges and universities, writing conferences, synagogues, and book fairs. Featured in two documentaries, he has been a panelist at London's Jewish Film Festival and is widely sought after as a panelist, moderator and keynoter at conferences. Raphael has been writing full-time since 1988 and is the book critic for National Public Radio's "The Todd Mundt Show" and "Mysteries" columnist for *The Detroit Free Press*. He also reviews for *Jerusalem Report, The Forward, The Washington Post* & *The Ft. Worth Star-Telegram*.